Inklings Book 2020

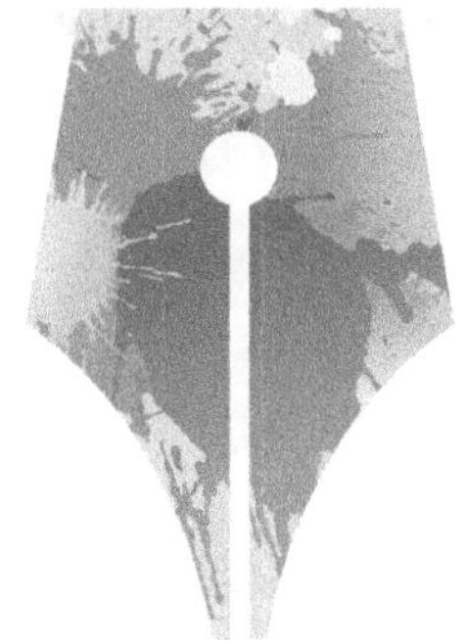

The following youth authors contributed their short stories and poems to this anthology.

Diya Balaji

Claire Belcourt

Steven Cavros

Jubilee Close

Victoria Cui

Aidan Felt

Ynez Foxe-Robertson

Declan Greer

Claire Guo

Suhani Gupta

Trisha Iyer

Ayana Kadkol

Karina Knowles

Emma Long

Audrina Quiroz

Reagan Ricker

Shreya Sujit

Lila Tierney

Pierce Wright

Anna Yang

Thank you to the following mentors for contributing editorial guidance and letters.

Bronté Bettencourt

Philomena Block

Alex Doherty

Malar Ganapathiappan

Melanie Heuiser Hill

Jamie Kallio

Ailynn Knox-Collins

Naomi Kinsman

Tasslyn Magnusson

Desiree Middleton

Melody Reed

Beth Spencewood

Elizabeth Verdick

Megan White

Kristi Wright

Cover illustration by Ting Chang
Edited by Naomi Kinsman

Printed in the USA
First Printing: August 2020
ISBN: 978-0-9981849-8-2

Contents

Thank you to our Collaborating Artists!

John David Anderson	Jill Davis	Daria Peoples-Riley
Kerry Aradhya	Mandy Davis	Mitali Perkins
Katy Bartkowski	Christine Dowd	Shannon Price
Rebecca Behrens	Sharon M. Draper	Helen Pyne
Ashley Herring Blake	Lisa Greenwald	Raina Telgemeier
Scott Bly	Marilyn Hilton	Elizabeth Verdick
Joanna Ho Bradshaw	Ann Jacobus	Ashley Walker
Dave Butler	Heidi Lang	Pam Watts
Kheryn Callender	Lea Lyon	Kristi Wright
Ernesto Cisneros	Beth McMullen	Anne Young
Kim Culbertson	Patricia Newman	

At Society of Young Inklings, we mentor youth authors because we know learning to think creatively opens every door. We offer game-based resources, online courses, and one-on-one mentorships to help youth authors move the big ideas from their heads and hearts onto the page. Find out more about our programs, including the annual *Inklings Book* Contest, at www.younginklings.org.

Foreword

Dear Reader,

In this, our twelfth annual Inklings Book, you'll experience laughter, heartache, magic, surprise, and above all, hope. The twenty 3rd – 9th grade authors featured in this anthology are this year's Inklings Book contest winners; inspired writers who've poured their hearts and creativity onto the page.

When readers see a published piece, it's tempting to think the words came out polished and perfect in first–draft form. However, drafting is only the beginning. I'm probably not telling you anything you don't know. Most likely, you, like many of our readers, are a *writer*, too. One of the most supportive gifts writers can give one another is the story behind their writing. How do initial ideas shape up into masterpieces, like the ones you'll read here?

Okay, yes, the answer is *revision*, but not just any kind of revision. At Society of Young Inklings, we don't pick through our manuscripts for errors, searching for everything that's wrong. Instead, we consider an amazing piece of writing an opportunity to take our thinking and innovation to the next level. That's what artists—and of course, authors are artists who create with the medium of words—do.

Here's how revision works in the Inklings Book process. First, our applicants polish and refine their work before they submit. They think about what effect they'd like their piece to have on their readers. Do they want their readers to laugh? To cry? To think? How can they use their characters, settings, word choice, rhythm, tone, or plot to create that outcome?

Once a piece is chosen for the Inklings Book, youth authors meet with a pro mentor. With their mentor, youth authors focus on one element as they revise, such as character development or metaphor. Instead of looking for what's wrong in the piece, they look for opportunities to exaggerate what's working well. Each piece comes even more fully to life through this collaboration. Many of our youth authors say what they like best about the Inklings Book process is working with someone who cares as deeply about their work as they do. That's pure creative joy.

Alongside each of the stories and poems in this book, you'll find letters from our mentors about the revision strategies used, plus an interview with the youth author about their revision process and insight they gained. You'll find many tips and tools you can take away for your own projects. And of course, the heart of this book is each of these twenty phenomenal stories and poems.

It's always a joy to edit the Inklings Book, and to see the anthology come together. I love the range of genres, the way I'm laughing one minute and tearing up the next as I read my way through. This year's book is a particular treat. Savor the reading, and may our collection also spark creative ideas for your writing, as well.

Happy Reading!

Naomi Kinsman
INKLINGS BOOK EDITOR

An Enticing Opening

Ayana Kadkol collaborated with mentor, Melody Reed, on a revision of *The Zoo Exhibit* to make the beginning of the story so enticing that it draws readers into the action from the very first words.

Dear Reader,

The Zoo Exhibit is mystery with a bit of fantasy. Like other mystery stories, *The Zoo Exhibit* is filled with twist and turns, as it follows Peter who takes a trip to his local zoo to see his favorite animal. Peter has visited Ash, a Bengal tiger several times, however, this trip turns out quite different.

"What's going to happen next?" is the question that keeps mystery readers reading and a writer needs to get them asking it from the very beginning. Ayana has created a strong plot arc in her writing piece. Because Ayana did so well with pacing the suspense, we decided to focus on creating **an enticing opening**, to bring the strength of the her middle and ending of the story to her beginning.

Ayana and I identified how she could reshape her opening, which was already filled with character introduction, interesting description, and pieces of backstory. By rearranging narrative into action, internal thought into dialogue and sprinkling setting throughout, she could create

a strong scene, which will pique the reader's curiosity.

The first line, "On Saturday, Peter and his family set off to the zoo," became "What are we going to do when we get there?" asked Peter. One sentence tells us a fact, the other leaves us wondering—who, what, where, and why.

Next time you read a new story, after the first page, stop and ask yourself—what question(s) have caught your attention? What can't you wait to find out? Notice how the author grabbed your interest and try a similar approach in your next story.

Congratulations, Ayana. Thank you for sharing your work.

Happy Writing!
Melody Reed

Melody Reed is a writer, teacher, and young adult library reference assistant who has way too many books than her house can hold. As a writing mentor through the Society of Young Inklings, she finds joy in sharing the knowledge she has learned from all the generous writers who have touched her life. Melody earned a bachelor's degree in Science from the University of St. Francis and an MFA in Writing for Children and Young Adults from Hamline University. When she is not working with young writers or young readers, she enjoys taking nature walks looking for inspiration. She is currently working on several projects, which include science. She lives in Chicago with her family and two precious little dogs.

Ayana Kadkol

Ayana Kadkol is a horse-obsessed third grader. In her free time, Ayana likes to ride horses, sketch horses and cats, read books, and—of course, she loves to write! Ayana is also very passionate about the environment. She helps it as much as possible everyday by reusing and recycling.. When she grows up, Ayana wishes to own a horse and become a bestselling author. Her favorite book is *The Door by the Staircase* by Katherine Marsh. Her other favorites include the *Harry Potter*, *Percy Jackson*, *Dragon Rider*, *Warriors*, and *Wings of Fire* books.

Melody Reed: How do you come up with your stories?
Ayana Kadkol: Usually, I write when I am bored and have nothing to do. My ideas are better then because now I have something to do. I never force myself to write. I usually start with a setting or a character and build up a plot based on the setting.

Q: How long have you been working on this story?
A: I started writing this story when I was about 6 years old. I left it in my notebook, and when I was old enough to submit to the contest, I improved it and sent it in.

Q: Why do you enjoy writing?
A: I enjoy writing because it is a fun thing to do and it helps me express my ideas on a paper which turns into a story.

Q: What do you like to write about?
A: I like to write about the environment and animals. I do not like to write fantasy. My stories are usually realistic fiction.

Q: Who do enjoy sharing your stories with?

A: I like sharing my stories with my parents and my best friend who also likes to write. We also like to write stories together.

The Zoo
Exhibit

by

Ayana Kadkol

"What are we going to do when we get there?" Peter asked.

"The answer to that is, we're going to see the parrots," said Dad.

"The parrots? Those birds are lame! All they do is sit around and squawk like Penny," Peter exclaimed.

"No, they squawk like you!" retorted Penny.

"Cut it out you two, we're going to see the parrots," said Mom, looking sternly into Peter's green eyes.

"But, can we not start by seeing the tiger, Ash. Please?" begged Peter.

"NO, spoiled brat. Not this time," put in Penny, Peter's tall older sister who had a permanent frown and, of course, a disliking for Peter.

Penny often woke up early. Sometimes Peter wondered if she woke up early just to put on her frown. When he shared his "suspicions" with his father, he just laughed.

When they arrived at the zoo, everyone got out and stretched their legs. They bought tickets at the front gate and went through the arched opening. They headed towards an old, cracked fountain and discussed where they were going to go.

"Okay. First, we're seeing the parrots, then the foxes, then the koalas, then we see the other animals, and lastly, we see the tiger," said Penny, shooting a nasty grin at Peter.

"That's not fair!" burst out Peter. Then you'll be the one getting everything you want."

"No, it'll be for a change because usually when we come to the zoo, we go to the tiger first, and you're the only one who wants to see the tiger first."

They squabbled for a while, and when their parents got fed up with this, they asked Peter to go off and see the tiger by himself.

Peter walked to the tiger exhibit by himself, passing the parrot exhibit where his family was admiring a bright red parrot. Peter went on and reached the predator exhibit.

He walked in and saw Ash. Wet and slick with his fur sticking to his body, Ash was crouched in his exhibit. It looked like he had just come out of the pool. He sat down and began to draw his paws over his ears. About halfway through his grooming, Peter got bored of looking at Ash licking himself and decided to catch up with his family.

As he started walking back towards where he thought his family might be, he got distracted when he saw an exhibit he had never seen before. It was called *Creatures of the Deep Sea*. Peter thought it was strange that this exhibit had no signs nor any information about the exhibit or the creatures in it. Thinking it wouldn't hurt if he stayed away for five more minutes, Peter walked in and the brown door squeaked as he pushed it open. It was very dark inside and there were lots of ancient fish fossils and skeletons in the exhibit. Peter whirled around and stifled a yelp. Behind him, there was a tank full of strange creatures

staring at him. Out of curiosity, Peter pressed a glowing, green button on the wall. Peter expected some information to show up on some screen on the wall. Instead, suddenly the glass from the tank slid down and water gushed out around him, drenching his clothes and filling his nostrils. The door to the exhibit widened and became the glass instead. Peter thumped on the glass with his fist in a vain attempt to get out, and that was all he remembered until he blacked out.

When Peter awoke, he looked at the glass and what he saw sent a huge wave of shock over him. There were fish swimming around him, and he could breathe perfectly fine in the cold, dark water. His reflection in the glass was hard to believe.

He now had a long tail, creepy eyes and sharp teeth. Peter had turned into an eel.

Peter thumped wildly at the glass with his tail in an attempt to free himself. He heard a raspy voice behind him.

"Stop it," the voice said. "There is no way to get out. Believe me, I have tried. We are all trapped in here."

Meanwhile, outside, his parents were frantically looking for him.

Penny, on the other hand, was ecstatic and sang, "*Finally*, this world is right, the little nuisance is gone!"

Peter's parents ignored her and set off looking for Peter in the zoo. Minutes, hours, and eventually days passed with no clue of Peter's disappearance. The police had to call off the search, and sadly, Peter's parents had no choice but to move on.

While the outside world had given up all hope of finding him, inside the dark aquarium, Peter had still not given up. He poked his nose and tail into every nook and cranny that he swam by and tried to find the button that turned him into an eel in the first place. Peter started looking under each rock, and one

of them had a hole underneath it. He tried to go down the hole, but it was a dead end. He tried burrowing down but hit cement. He thought and thought-and soon became upset. The thought that he may never be able to leave crept into his mind. He wondered if he would have to live in this tank till the end of his days. He didn't want to die as a fish.

Die! Peter suddenly thought. No one wanted a dead fish in their aquarium. If Peter played dead, the next time someone came to feed them, they would remove him, thinking that he was actually dead.

The next day, Peter put his plan into action when a tall, gangly man walked in to feed the fish. Peter quickly lay on his side and closed his eyes, not daring to twitch a muscle. The man dropped some kind of hard, brown pellets into the tank and then noticed that Peter was not moving at all, neither did it look like he was sleeping.

He thought that Peter was dead. He didn't know that Peter was playing dead, though. The man thought that Peter was actually dead, and he was disgusted. Reaching into the tank with a hairy hand, the man slowly lifted Peter out of the tank by his tail. Peter tried his best not to squirm and wriggle as the man lifted him out of the tank and threw him out in the bushes outside the exhibit. A few hours later, Peter felt a strange sensation going through his body. Slowly, he turned back into a kid—a wet kid, but nevertheless, a kid.

When Peter finally got out, he ran home and rang the doorbell to the utter joy of his parents and surprisingly, his sister too. His sister was actually the happiest of all, and so, she hugged Peter's short, skinny frame, and ruffled his already messy brown hair. No one asked him why he was soaking wet, they were just glad to have him back. Peter's parents asked him where he had been all the while, but Peter said that he had no memory of what had happened.

Peter started to get back to his regular schedule. The next day, he slept in, and when he woke up, he ran as quickly as possible to *Alder Middle*, his school, and ran into the classroom.

He was 20 minutes late. Mrs. Vencher gave him a smile. For once, she was glad to have him back. Things were turning out different at school. For instance, Peter had a quiz. The topic was The Deep Sea. Peter had not studied at all, nor was he interested in sea creatures. He scribbled down all the answers indifferently and was surprised to find that he was the first to finish.

Later in the day, his mom got a call from Mrs. Vencher that Peter got 100% on the quiz, and that she needed to talk to his mom about it. Peter's mom was very glad, because usually Mrs. Vencher called her because Peter gotten a *bad grade* on his quiz.

Another such instance was the swim meet where Peter had been asked to represent his school because the top two swimmers in the school were out sick. Peter surprised himself and the coach when he won first place and set a new record for the school. The next few swim meets were all like this where Peter was breaking records and winning first place. This prompted his father to ask him how he was suddenly swimming so well. Peter himself was not sure but blurted out that things had been different for him after his visit to the zoo, especially the visit to the *Creatures of the Deep Sea* exhibit. His dad was surprised because, all this while, Peter had never mentioned anything about the zoo visit nor did he seem to remember anything from that visit. Peter's dad found it weird as he did not seem to recollect seeing the *Creatures of the Deep Sea* exhibit on the zoo brochure.

Out of curiosity, they decided to look it up on the internet. While searching on the internet, they found no results matching their search. While Peter was positive that he had visited that exhibit, he was not sure why it was not showing up in the search. Even though Peter described the location to his father and told him that it was in the northwest corner of the zoo, his father still didn't believe him, and Peter made his father drive him to the zoo to show him. To his surprise, the exhibit wasn't there. Peter's dad found a zookeeper,

and he asked him whether there was an exhibit called *Creatures of the Deep Sea.* The zookeeper shook his head.

Peter said, "Well, while I was there, I saw a tall man with big hands and a beard walk up to feed the fish."

The zookeeper said that none of the people who worked at the zoo were very tall. "Actually, kid, I'm the tallest person who works here," he said.

Peter surveyed the man, and he wasn't very tall himself. Feeling disappointed, Peter followed his dad into the car.

A few weeks later, when Peter's dad was reading the paper, he jumped up and spilled coffee all over himself, burning his hand and staining his red-checkered pajamas. He had a shocked expression on his face because the headlines on the front page said that the police had found some clues in their investigation of the mysterious disappearance of the town's children. The clues led to the northwest corner of the zoo and the trail went cold.

THE END

Sensory Detail

Karina Knowles worked with mentor, Kristi Wright, on using sensory detail to evoke her character's memories and emotions in *I Speak for the Bees*.

Dear Reader:

I Speak for the Bees is a gorgeous tale about young Maya on her annual summer visit to her grandparents who are fruit growers and beekeepers. For the first time ever, she's visiting without her older sister, who is spending the summer with friends instead. But there's also a mystery afoot—the bees are disappearing and therefore are producing less honey. Karina has steeped her story in beautiful language and sensory moments, resulting in both authenticity and reading pleasure.

As an editor, I had a hard time identifying a revision focus for our mentorship together. Because Karina's story exists in the world of orchards and harvests, bee hives and honey, all of which naturally beg the writer to overload the reader with a sensory experience, I finally decided to ask her to double down on her use of descriptive language.

In my editorial letter, I challenged Karina to look for more opportunities to add **sensory detail** and also to consider how she might use sensory moments to evoke memory or possibly to trigger emotion. It's a known scientific fact that there's a strong tie between our senses and both memory and emotions.

However, I also reminded Karina that ultimately, she needed to please herself with her revision. I wanted her to use our discussion as inspiration, not dictation. I asked her not to try to please me, but to please herself.

And here's where the magic happened. In Karina's revision, she did find multiple opportunities for additional sensory detail, but the majority of her changes had to do with adding more memories—because that was the editorial suggestion that resonated the most. Sometimes those memories were obviously triggered by Maya's senses, but sometimes the connection was less obvious. And that didn't matter! Karina's tale was significantly enriched by all her changes.

So, here's my advice to you as writers of your *own* tales. When you receive editorial suggestions, whether from teachers, peers, family, or mentors, sit with those ideas for a bit. Think about which excite you and feel true to your story, and which inspire you to dig in and experiment. Don't just make changes because someone tells you to, but rather, take ownership of your work and look for ways to improve it that delight you.

Yes, adding sensory detail can enhance the beauty and authenticity of your story, and it can help you to trigger an important memory in your main character or bring them to a deeply emotional moment. But only if you stay true to your own evolving vision of your story. Embrace advice, but never forget to always tell the tale that only you can tell.

Happy Writing,

Kristi Wright

Kristi Wright writes picture books and middle grade novels. Her goal as a writer is to give children a sense of wonder, a hopefulness about humanity, and a belief in their future. Her indie-published futuristic middle grade series, *The Basker Twins in the 31st Century*, raises funds and awareness for the childhood-onset disease, Friedreich's ataxia. She's an active volunteer for the Society of Children's Books Writers and Illustrators (SCBWI) and assistant editor for KidLitCraft.com, a blog on the craft of writing children's literature. She lives in Northern California with her dear husband, one sweet but wacky dog, and two fiendishly clever cats. She's a writer by day and a ukulele player by night.

Find her at kristiwrightauthor.com and on Twitter @KristiWrite.

Karina Knowles

Karina Knowles is twelve years old and entering 7th grade at a Montessori school in the Bay Area. She loves reading and writing stories and poems. She also enjoys biking, rock climbing and art from building to painting. One day, she would love to visit all the national parks, to photograph and paint the endless variety of wildlife and nature there. She would like to dedicate this story to her older sister Anika. (And maybe her two adorable cats!)

Kristi Wright: What inspired you to write *I Speak for the Bees?*
Karina Knowles: I like biking to the local fruit orchard in my neighborhood so that was part of it. But, when I really had the idea I was walking around my block and saw how few pollinators there were. Then, that sparked a story.

Q: When you submitted your story to Young Inklings, you mentioned that you really liked how your main character finds her voice through poetry. What made you think of that?
A: Well, my first thought was that Maya used her voice through painting, but later, I realized that I'm using my voice by writing this story, so why not have Maya write a poem? So, I decided that was more fitting.

Q: Which is your favorite line in your poem? Why?
A: I think it would be "So let's ALL speak for the bees" because that is the whole point of the story.

Q: How did you feel about focusing on sensory descriptive language for your revision?

A: I think it was helpful to add sensory details for Maya's memories of Clara and herself. That way Clara can be a bigger part of the story and Maya has more of a reason to accept Ali at the end.

Q: Did you learn anything from this revision process that you can use as you write your next story?

A: I learned how the revision process works! Also, how to incorporate more memory into a story.

Q: What advice would you give other writers about revision?

A: Don't be shy to say "No, I don't want that." It is your choice how you want to revise your story.

Q: You've been submitting work to the Young Inklings Contest for many years now. What do you feel you've learned from the experience?

A: That just because your story doesn't get published, doesn't mean your story is bad. I also learned more from the revision letters I got.

Q: What are you writing now?

A: I've recently started planning a story that includes magic and a mission.

Q: What are some of your favorite books?

A: I like too many books to count, from many genres! Fantasy, fiction, historical fiction... etc. Five of my favorites are: *The Silver Sister* series, *The Land of Stories* series, the *Harry Potter* series, *More to the Story*, and *Inside Out and Back Again*.

Q: What other things do you like to do besides write and read books?

A: I love to build with recycled boxes, climb rocks and trees, and paint nature scenes, but most of all I love the outdoors and animals.

I Speak for the Bees

by

Karina Knowles

I glance out the car window at the stretch of hills rolling off into the horizon, thinking of the wonderful relaxing days ahead. It's summer at last! I'm spending the summer as usual on Lola and Pop's farm. Lola and Pop are my grandparents, who live on a small orchard and bee farm. They grow fruit and harvest honey for a living. I've visited every summer since—well, forever. I love it there, enjoying Lola's homemade Mexican dishes, harvesting fruit and honey with Pop, and biking with my big sister Clara.

But this summer is going to be different: Clara is getting to spend her vacation at her new friend's cabin in Tahoe. I wish I had a best friend like she does. We have always been so close, but right now she feels so distant.

Around the bend I spot the familiar greeting sign, *Welcome to Valle de Frutas*. As my mom pulls to a stop in Lola and Pop's driveway, I jump out of the car and run to my smiling grandparents with open arms.

The next morning, I wake up to delicious smells wafting from downstairs. Lola has made her famous arepas for breakfast. Yum! I quickly dress and fly down the stairs, but before I enter the kitchen, I hear Lola and Pop talking with my parents in an agitated tone. Poking my head through the door, I listen to the conversation.

"The bees' numbers have dwindled this year. There's less honey every month. And with the bees disappearing, the income is lower," Pop says, furrowing his brow.

"That's terrible," my Dad replies. "How is this happening?"

"We don't know." Lola sighs as the arepas sizzle on the grill. "But Dave, our farm hand, is trying to solve it and we have a pretty good idea now."

At that moment Lola catches me eavesdropping and waves me into the room. She heaps three steaming arepas onto my plate and passes me the beans.

"*Buenos días*, Maya!" Lola says with her warm smile. "You don't need to hide, we were going to tell you anyway!"

"Sorry," I say, my mouth full of tortilla. "Can I help?"

"*No sé*, there isn't much we can do until we know what is happening to them. But you can go to Dave's after breakfast with Pop and check on the bees." Lola adds with a grin, "I'm glad you want to help!"

"*Sí*, Lola is right, we need to find out what is happening to them first," Pop agrees. "Why don't you help your parents pack up and then we can go? Dave wants you to meet someone."

I agree and finish my last bite of arepa as I head upstairs with Mom and Dad. My parents only stayed the first night because they have to work back home in Sacramento.

Later, as I wave goodbye to them, my heart starts to sink. Even though I'll have Lola and Pop, it still will be a lonely summer without Clara.

Now that Mom and Dad have gone, Pop and I head out to Dave's. We walk along a well-used path that curves around the peach and apricot trees. Honeysuckle bushes line the path with lilac blooms. The sweet aroma of nectar floats all around.

We pass by the bee hives, and I can't help wondering why the bees have been disappearing. *Maybe they got sick, or could they have lost their queen and abandoned their hive?*

When we arrive at Dave's, I spot a girl with long blonde hair and eyes sparkling in excitement.

"This is Ali," Dave announces with a smile. "She's my niece who just arrived a week ago from Chicago. She will be staying here for the summer and is twelve like you."

"Hi, I'm Maya." My voice is quivery, and I can feel my face turning pink. I'm shy around people I meet.

"Maya!" Ali exclaims, waving her hand. "Uncle Dave has told me all about you! I'm so glad there will be someone my age staying here for the summer, too!"

I feel the same way, but don't say so.

"Yeah," I mumble instead.

"Well, what are we waiting for? Get suited up and we will go harvest some honey!" Pop declares.

Each of us slips on white beekeeper suits and gloves, finally placing a netted mask over our faces and heads. Then Pop grabs a frame lifter tool and the smoker to calm the bees so we can access the honey.

When we arrive at the beehives, Pop opens the lid of the first hive. A noisy cloud of bees emerges from within. The bees dance in the air like a flock

of birds before settling down again. Using the smoker to clear off the bees, Pop next pries out a frame full of amber honey, inspecting it carefully.

"Nice!" he finally exclaims. "Fresh cappings, this one's good."

After collecting the honey frames, we head back to Dave's house to set up and begin harvesting the honey. In the large kitchen, Pop and Dave scrape off the wax cappings, the wax falling into a bowl to be strained later. Next comes the fun part. Ali and I place the frames full of honey into the extractor and take turns spinning the honey out of the frames. As the frames spin round and round, I can't help feeling a pang of sadness, remembering the first time Pop taught Clara and me how to harvest honey all those summers ago. Together.

"Maya, look!" Ali's voice brings me back into the present.

When all the honey has been extracted, I watch it pour into a waiting jar. The honey sparkles in the afternoon sun. I spoon some into my mouth—it's warm, fresh from the hive.

"Less honey than last year." Pop rubs his chin and paces the floor. I can tell he is worried—and so am I.

After the five of us finish Lola's delicious lunch of fresh-squeezed lemonade and quesadillas, I ask Pop if I can bike to the library. He says yes, if Ali would come with me, like Clara normally does.

"Great idea," says Ali. "Let's research what could be happening to the bees."

It's a 15-minute ride to the library in Cerritos, my grandparents' town. Ali borrows Clara's bike and helmet and we head off.

"See ya! Be safe!" Dave calls as we leave the driveway.

"Don't worry, Uncle Dave!" Ali replies. "Maya knows the town!"

That's true. I've biked to the library with Clara too many times to count, and I could bike there with my eyes closed. Even though she's not Clara, I guess Ali isn't so bad. Maybe we could be friends.

Round and round my wheels go to the rhythm of my pedals. The breeze is warm but not too hot yet, and I can hear little robins chirping in shady trees. I look back to see Ali just behind me. She is humming and an expression of happiness is written all over her face.

"Pretty, isn't it?" I offer.

"Oh, yes!"

A little way further, we turn a corner and slow to a stop in front of a quaint building, its paint fading from years of sunbathing. A small sign hangs from the door announcing: "Welcome to The Cerritos Town Library! Open Monday through Friday, 1 to 6 pm."

The library is my favorite place on earth. My getaway and worry-free world. As I open the door, a little bell jingles above me, signaling our entrance. The familiar smell of old books greets me. We spend the next hour pouring through every book on bees we can find.

Back home, we find Pop and Dave picking strawberries. I join them as Ali shares our research. "Uncle Dave, Mr. Garcia! Maya and I found these books about bees! They say that many are disappearing due to pesticides, herbicides and monocultures."

"Great! Those are good possibilities, but we can't be certain yet what ours are dealing with," Pop explains, placing a bright red strawberry into his basket. "Though it can't be monocultures, because we grow a large variety of crops."

"I think that pesticides could be a reason, even though our fruit is organic," Dave adds. "The Coopersons, our new neighbors, spray their fields. We saw the duster plane when you were gone. "

"So we can sue them?" I ask.

I sneak a strawberry into my mouth. It tastes as sweet as summer. Clara and I used to pick strawberries together, racing to fill our baskets.

"I'm sorry, Maya." Pop shakes his head. "It isn't illegal to use pesticides, but I'll go over and talk to them this evening. Maybe they don't know about our bee problem."

The next afternoon, Ali and I are sprawled out under a large, shady orange tree in the center of the orchard. Books and papers are scattered across the ground. Sunlight filters through the tree's canopy, warming my skin. The smooth trunk of the tree cools my back. It's mainly quiet except for the occasional call of a bird or the rumble of a truck speeding by.

I'm writing a poem about bees, letting myself feel free like a bee, my wings the paper and my soul the pen. I glance up from my notebook to see Ali reading while munching on an orange, its sticky juice dripping down her chin. I wonder how Ali feels about the whole "bee problem."

When Pop talked to the neighbors about stopping their use of pesticides, their response was: "No! You want pesky little bugs in your fruit? Have at it!" No matter how hard he tried, he couldn't get their stubborn minds to change. Pop says he'll try again when they cool off.

"Ali?" I ask. "What do you think we should do about the bees?"

"Huh? Dunno." Ali ignores me, too engaged in her book.

I sigh, thinking about the dilemma. If the bees were to disappear there

would be no honey and no more fruit. I remember when Clara and I would pick fresh berries near the creek together. We would always bake with them and sell our goods. All of a sudden it comes to me.

"That's it!" I declare, dropping my pencil. "We could make a bake sale for the bees!"

"Yeah!" Ali snaps out of her book. "Or we could organize a petition for the town council to ban the spraying of pesticides and herbicides in Cerritos!"

"Yeah! That's even better! Come on!"

We race into Lola and Pop's house, banging the screen door behind us.

After we explain the petition to Lola and Pop, Lola smiles. "I think that's a wonderful idea! Who would have thought of that! What do you think, José?"

"Hmm, it could work. Doesn't hurt to give it a try! When would we start collecting signatures?"

"How about we start on Sunday when we bring the harvest to the farmer's market?" Ali is practically jumping out of her seat.

I'm glad to see that she cares as much as I do.

"If we have enough signatures by then, we could present the petition to the Mayor at the Fourth of July parade!" I add. "Everyone will be there."

"I'll talk to Dave and see his thoughts about it. It could possibly work."

"Yes!" Ali and I shout at the same time and high five.

"Jinx!" Ali snorts, and soon we all are laughing. I think I've made a friend.

"In the meantime, come and help me make jam," invites Lola. "There is still a lot of work we need to do before the farmer's market!" Lola drags us into the kitchen, and we get to work. Deep purple juice bleeds over my cutting board as I smash the berries and I wonder, *Will I have to talk to strangers?*

My stomach flips at the mere thought.

"Did you get the kumquats and peaches?" Dave calls from the driver's seat of the old, mud-splattered pickup truck.

"Yep!" I heave two crates of kumquats, the last of the season, into the back of the truck.

Ali follows close behind with the peaches.

"Good. Then we are all set!" Dave says.

"Off to market!" Ali exclaims.

We climb into the jump seats of the truck, and Pop hops into the passenger seat. A dust cloud erupts as we fly down the road. I wave to Lola standing on the porch, and she waves back until we're out of sight. Lola has a bad leg, so she can't come. Instead, she'll stay home and make cookies and lemonade for us when we come back. Selling is harder than it looks.

When we arrive, we unload the truck and carry our harvest to a big table under one of the many rows of white canopies. Dave sets up the cashier box, while the rest of us lay out the produce, jam, and honey.

About a half an hour later, when we finish the setup, people start pouring into the market with bags in hand. Ali and I get ready to start the petition signing. We each hold a pen and a clipboard with petition papers.

"Oh!" A lady in a mint green shawl walks up to the stand, scanning the produce. "You have apricot jam! I'll take one apricot jam and five ripe peaches."

Pop bags up her items and Dave receives the cash.

Just as she's about to leave, Ali pipes up, "Excuse me, Mam, but before you go, would you like to sign our petition? We are trying to prevent the use of pesticides in Cerritos, because it's hurting the bees!"

Ali hands her the article that I wrote last night.

The woman reads it carefully and then responds, "Why not?" She fills out the form and returns the clipboard.

"Thank you kindly!" Ali calls after her.

I just whisper, "Thanks," under my breath.

"Maya!" Ali says, "You didn't say thank you!"

"I did," I insist, not wanting her to see that I'm shy.

"Whatever!" She rolls her eyes at me and I look down. "Here comes a nice old man. Why don't you ask him to sign the petition? All you have to do is ask him and then say thank you. Come on!" She pushes me over to him.

I try to speak, but all I can manage to croak is, "Sssign?"

The man looks at me weirdly and then moves on. My cheeks burn and I can feel Ali's eyes boring a hole right through the back of my head.

I prepare to get yelled at, but instead all Ali says is, "It's OK. I'll do the talking and you can just hand out the article."

I feel a huge wave of relief wash over me as we get back to work.

For the next two weeks, Ali and I bike back and forth from the town to the farm, each time coming home with a stack of signatures. Ali does most of the talking, but by the end I can at least ask them to sign.

One day in early July, when we come home with a particularly large stack, Lola is waiting for us in the kitchen with freshly squeezed lemonade and steaming churros.

"*Hola!* How was it today?"

"We've got plenty of names, so Ali and I think this was our last day." I sip my lemonade, the sweet, cold drink so refreshing after a long day in the sun.

"Already? It seems like you just started!" she laughs. "Are you ready to bring them to the parade tomorrow?"

"Yep," Ali sighs. "It's been a long week, but worth it!" Then Ali says goodbye and bikes back to Dave's house across the field.

After she leaves I talk to Lola. "Lola? Do I have to speak tomorrow?"

"It would be nice if you did, but if you don't feel comfortable, you don't have to." She sits down beside me, "You know Maya, I know you are quite the poet. And I know you've been writing about bees—I saw you last night. Maybe you can present it at the parade, but you don't—"

"No!" I cut her off. "Sorry, I'm just not ready to share my writing with the whole town."

That night I toss and turn, dreaming of an empty world without bees. I turn on my lamp and open my notebook. I've got to do this. I've got to do it for the bees.

We all wake up early to prepare for the parade. It's the biggest and best part of the summer! It's when we march from the library to City Hall for a big ceremony, near Mallard's Lake. Ali and I paint each other's faces with red, white, and blue stripes, like Clara and I used to do, before helping Lola pack lunch. Then we all pile into the truck, even Lola, who is making this special trip because no one in the town can miss the biggest day of the summer!

Before the parade starts, Lola pulls me aside and holds out my small, purple notebook, its cover worn from use.

"In case you change your mind," she winks. Then she exclaims, "Now look, the parade is starting!"

In front of the library, a big crowd has gathered. There are people holding banners, people eating ice cream, people face painting, and even people singing. I spot Uncle Sam, wearing his tall striped hat as the drums sound and the parade begins.

When we arrive at City Hall, the townspeople file into the rows of plastic folding chairs facing a large podium where Mayor Lee is standing. I take a seat near the front next to Ali, who is holding our stack of petition papers. I clutch my notebook close to my chest. As Mayor Lee's speech starts, I can't help wondering about my poem.

Is it good enough? Will people laugh? What if the petition doesn't work and all of our hives die off!?

"Ahem!" I'm interrupted by a loud, booming voice. "And now for a last-minute addition, we have the farm of *Valle de Frutas* presenting a petition."

Ali tugs on my arm. "Come on, this is our chance! Come on!"

Pop and Ali head up to the podium.

"Coming!" I call after her.

Lola squeezes my arm and whispers, "Hope you changed your mind! Remember, use your voice."

"I have," I say. "For the bees!"

"Good luck then! And remember what I said."

I smile, but as I reach the podium, I feel butterflies in my stomach. Ali speaks about our petition and Pop explains how important bees are. Then, we hand Mayor Lee the stack of signatures. The audience applauds politely as my palms begin to sweat. I hear Ali cheering me on. Now it's my turn, there's no turning back. I scan the rows of seats and find Lola beaming up at me.

Use your voice. Lola's words echo in my head.

Don't worry I will! I think, smiling back at her.

I take a deep breath and start to read my poem, my hands trembling.

"I Speak for the Bees

I speak for the bees, as one flies across blossoming fields

Enjoying the stretch of blue sky all around it.

I speak for the bees, as it lands on a bloom, sipping nectar and collecting

pollen

Resting on the soft pink petal beneath its fuzzy feet.

I speak for the bees, though it does not know it has done the flower a

service.

Soon an apple will take its place, for me to enjoy one day.

I speak for the bees, while in the hive it makes honey.

Maybe that amber liquid will sweeten my morning tea.

You see, we depend on bees for peaches so juicy, strawberries so sweet

and lemons so fresh.

We have the bees to thank for most everything we have on our plate.

Without them we're gone, too.

So please, help protect them, for they mean everything to you and me.

Hurting them is like hurting you.

So, let's ALL speak for the bees."

I hear an eruption of claps and whistles, then feel someone give me a big hug.

"You did it! Good job!" Ali shouts.

As I return to my seat, Lola smiles. "I knew you could do it!"

That night after dinner, Ali and I sit outside, on the porch eating flan. We can just see the beehives off in the distance, a silhouette against the ombre sky. Crickets sing their nighttime melody and I can faintly hear frogs croaking in Mallard's Lake. Clara and I used to look for constellations here, but that doesn't matter right now, I've got Ali.

Before dinner, the Coopersons called to inform us they had changed their minds and would stop using pesticides even if the town doesn't ban them. We were all thrilled, so Lola made flan to celebrate. We still don't know if the Mayor has decided to accept the policy or not, but I can rest on knowing that I've conquered my fear and made a new friend. Maybe I can get along without Clara after all. I think she would be proud of me. But, the most important thing is: I spoke for the bees.

Setting for Complication

Diya Balaji mentored with Melody Reed on a revision that focused on making the most of the setting to add even more tension to Diya's story, *Occento*.

Dear Reader,

Stories written as realistic fiction are bought to life through detailed descriptions. *Occento* is an excellent example of this truth. *Occento* depicts how Anisha Cala Ahmed and her beloved Baba deal with the death of her Mama very differently and when Anisha reaches for her dream, the two bond in a profound way.

Diya's story is filled with many wonderful descriptions of character development through internal thought and emotions. The reader quickly cares about Anisha and builds a connection with her. Because Diya did so well with these elements, we decided to build on her strength and focus on using **setting for complication** to increase the tension in her writing.

Diya and I sought out lines where a few words here and there, would strengthen the emotional experience. One of the obstacles Anisha faced was practicing her singing at home, which was in the basement

of snobby Madam Atoosa. Diya made it clear Madam Atoosa didn't appreciate her singing. But she realized she could do more to get the point across. She added "It was frigid and echoed a lot. As for Madam Atoosa, she never appreciated music, especially singing. It didn't help that the walls were paper thin, and she could hear music more than ever." Now the reader can see why this is a complication to Anisha reaching her dream of participating in the singing contest, Occento.

One way to find locations in a story which could enhance difficulty in the character getting what they want, is to highlight every type of setting detail with a marker. Ask yourself, "Do I have plenty places colored?" carefully examine if you could cause further problems for your character by adding bits of setting details to those locations.

Congratulations, Diya. Thank you for sharing your writing.

I wish you well on your writing journey!

Melody Reed

Melody Reed is a writer, teacher, and young adult library reference assistant who has way too many books than her house can hold. As a writing mentor through the Society of Young Inklings, she finds joy in sharing the knowledge she has learned from all the generous writers who have touched her life. Melody earned a bachelor's degree in Science from the University of St. Francis and an MFA in Writing for Children and Young Adults from Hamline University. When she is not working with young writers or young readers, she enjoys taking nature walks looking for inspiration. She is currently working on several projects, which include science. She lives in Chicago with her family and two precious little dogs.

Diya Balaji

Diya Balaji is a fifth grader who lives in Redmond Washington. She loves to read, cook, play basketball and act. Since first grade, she has been writing short stories. She loves writing because it takes her to a whole new world. Some of her favorite book series include *Spy School*, *Harry Potter*, and *Percy Jackson*.

Melody Reed: Why do you enjoy writing?

Diya Balaji: I enjoy writing because I think it is an art to engineer something that can have people visualize an event or scene down to the last detail. I also like to write, as I can be whisked away to faraway places, and I can choose where I want to go, while being at home.

Q: When did you start writing?

A: I started writing when I was in second grade. I wrote and illustrated a picture book. It was about a girl with a magic music box that can send her anywhere she likes. A year later, I wrote a bedtime story book for my brother (starring him) when he was born. Also, sometimes I like to converse in "book talk", which narrates what's happening around me in a third person- limited format.

Q: How did you get the idea for this story?

A: It was struggle and failure book report time at my school, and I thought that for my story, I could build off of that theme, and challenge myself with writing something a little more serious. Most of the previous stories I've written

were on a lighter tone, and I wanted to try something different. I decided to go for the plot first, as I think it's easiest to shape the story around it. I liked the themes of "following your dream" and "struggle and closure."

Q: What changed when you revised for using setting for complication?

A: After using setting details for complication, my story improved tremendously, because it allows you to see a clearer and more detailed picture, which is one of my favorite things about writing. I now can visualize my story much better, and I hope you can too!

Q: What advice do you offer Young Inklings who don't like revising all that much?

A: My advice is that revising doesn't mean that your story is a bad one, and that it needs to be completely altered. It means that your story is good, and it has so much potential, that others can see that there is a way to make this a stronger story. Through this process, you will realize that one of the main things that a story needs after it's written, is fresh eyes to make it even better.

Occento

by

Diya Balaji

I sighed in pleasure after the last note of my song, a fifteen-second-high C. The Thursday evening sunshine streamed in through the window, adding to my peace. When you are singing a song, you feel so exhilarated and euphoric.

"Like a dog with two tails," Mama used to say, smiling.

"Why would a dog be happy if he had two tails?" I had ventured. "Then he would be so … different."

Mama looked out the window into the stormy clouds, a faraway look in her eyes. "There's nothing wrong with being different, *Anisha Ma*. You know what they say, *in order to be irreplaceable, one must be different.*" She suddenly snapped out of her reverie. "Now eat your Ice Cream," she exclaimed, catching a drop that almost fell off my cone.

Did I notice? No. I was too busy gaping wide-mouthed at Mama, listening to her quote these words of wisdom. I didn't understand what she was talking about. To this day, in my wise ten-year-old state of mind, I still don't. But what I wouldn't give to hear those words again.

"Anisha!"

"Coming Baba!" I exclaimed quickly and then ran to the living room.

Baba was seated at the small spindly kitchen table, paying bills. He looked worn and tired, and worry lines creased his forehead. He has looked like that ever since Mama died five months ago, of cancer. I wish I could help him. I tried a lot, but it never seems to work.

When Mama and I used to sing, Baba would thump his hand against his knee, keeping to the *taal*, his eyes sparkling like a thousand smiles were lit up in them. But these days, when I sing, he just sags. Sometimes at night, I go to our tiny kitchen for a glass of water, and I hear him crying. He tries to hide it, but I know he does. And I can do nothing to help.

"Anisha, please be a little quieter. Madam Atoosa complained."

Madam Atoosa was a snobby lady whose basement we lived in. I still don't know how of all the basements in Redmond, Washington State, we landed in this one. It was frigid and echoed a lot. As for Madam Atoosa, she never appreciated music, especially singing. It didn't help that the walls were paper-thin, and she could hear music more than ever. After Mama died, she had been especially foul about my singing. But I suspect Baba is also closer minded about my singing because it's too painful a reminder of Mama. It soothes me when I sing, because it feels like Mama is still with me. I guess Baba doesn't feel that way.

"Okay Baba," I agreed, trying to be cheerful.

"Thanks,"

"Baba, please, may I ..."

"Anisha," His tone was stern and a bit sorrowful. " Again, you know that after Mama passed, I have been working double shifts to make ends meet. How can we pay fifty dollars to get you into that singing contest?"

"But Baba, I can work! Maybe at a store, or raking somebody's lawn, I don't know, but I'll work!"

"I can't let you out alone, Anisha. We already lost Mama ... I can't bear it if something happened to you." He took a deep, shaky breath, and when he looked up, his eyes were shining. "I am sorry, Anisha, but I can't let you do this."

"I understand, Baba." I replied quietly.

I ran to my room as fast as my skinny legs could carry me, over the creaky floor, so he wouldn't see the tears that my furiously blinking eyes were trying to hold back.

"One, two, Aah!" My best friend Kari let out a shout of fright as an egg came crashing down on his head.

He had been juggling three raw ones, and he fumbled. One cracked in one hand, one in the other, and one came SPLAT, on his head. Egg dripped down from him onto the sidewalk on the way home from the park, where we played every Friday. I noticed they made cool shapes as they fell, like suns and rainbows, even one resembling a unicorn!

I laughed. "And *somebody* said that they were an *expert* at juggling eggs."

He put out an open hand to reveal all the slimy egg goo. *Even that looked like a cupcake.*

"They say that raw egg makes you better at singing, he teased. "Care to try some?"

He must have seen something in my face change, because he suddenly grew serious." Hey, you'll find a way into the contest. You're Anisha the great. It will work out."

Kari knew me. He had helped me practice, singing along with me, or being chorus when there was nobody. He comforted me when Mama died. He made me laugh even when I didn't want to, which made me realize what I wanted to do was laugh more.

"Thanks, same to you and your eggs," I answered innocently.

"Hey!" he yelled behind me as I took off toward my house.

I could still tell he was smiling, though.

As I walked alone to my house, I noticed a piece of paper stuck to a strong, beautiful tree with smooth bark. As soon as I saw it, I immediately knew what it was. A flyer for the singing contest of my dreams, Occento. I had wanted to be in this contest for about a year. I had watched as the winners received their trophies tears streaming down their faces. I wanted to be like that too. Mama had promised to take me. She promised ... She had helped me prepare. But now, we were just too poor with Mama gone, and only Baba to work as a cashier at the local Balance Mart on the highway, where weather beaten hitchhikers were the only customers.

I looked at the torn, battered flyer that was my ticket to the contest longingly. It was going to happen on Sunday morning, which was in two days. It called for all the people who auditioned and got in to participate in the final contest. I had gotten in. But we just were too poor to pay for entering the contest.

A tsunami of passion and longing welled up in me. I thought of Mama. It had been her dream to see me up there on that stage with the multicolored lights. I had to do this. For me. For Mama. But what would Baba say? He would be scared when he realized that I had gone by myself, and by no doubt, angry that I had taken sixty dollars from the savings closet. But he would be so happy if I won, I know he would. I knew doing this was the right thing.

"Hello?" This is Anisha Cala Ahmed. You invited me to Occento. I wanted to tell you ... that I'm in."

The next day was terrible. I was a nervous wreck. My knee kept bouncing up and down and hitting the desk in all my classes, and Mrs. Lopez, the nicest teacher, lectured me in front of the whole class! I was forced to limp from one dull class to another, with a throbbing pain in my knee. I saw

Kari looking at me inquisitively, but I couldn't say anything, because I knew he would protest. I mean, he wouldn't want me walking for an hour alone outside at 5 am! I could think about nothing but the contest. I was nervous not about the singing, but what I had to do the next day.

That night, I tried to cheerfully bid good night to Baba, and hugged him extra hard. Then I retired to my room, fearing what was about to come my way.

4:00, my alarm said. I had nervously waited and had only pretended to sleep. I was feverishly steeling myself for the most dangerous and guilt-arousing part of my life. It was time. It was time to go into the savings closet.

I silently crept out of my room and tried to close the door softly. Being an old door, it creaked, I swear fifty times louder. I winced and looked around, seeing if Baba had woken.

Nope.

I kept sliding towards the closet furtively. I finally reached the closet. I opened the box with a hidden stash of money. It wasn't much, only about two hundred dollars, but it still was the most money I've ever seen. The prospect of stealing a quarter of it, plus an extra ten for provisions, made me quake with guilt.

I only brought a hairbrush with me. I was going to be on stage. I needed to have combed hair. I stepped outside in the cool, fresh night air. It was time.

The stadium was only an hour away by walk. It started at 6:00 in the morning. I checked my old battered watch. I would be there half an hour to the show. It was a peaceful walk, not on the road. I took the more serene route. It felt tranquil, with the wind slowly and rhythmically swaying the trees. Mama and I had walked here together many times. I felt at peace with the world for the first time Mama had died.

Each tree seemed to be whispering their encouragement, each gust of soft wind seemed to be pushing me forward, and each chirp of the crickets who dared to punctuate the silence of the night told me one thing. If they were so daring as to break the silent night, then I could break the fear I had for stealing and going against Baba's will to sing. But that's the problem. *It's not just to sing.* This is my life's dream, and I'm giving it away so soon? I can't do that! I pictured Mama's face, her determined smile and her comforting arm around me, promising that I'd be up on that stage one day. I couldn't let my dream—Mama's dream—go so easily.

I held my head high, said loudly "I *will* get there and sing, if it's the last thing I do!" and walked off.

Forty-five minutes later, I was quite the contrary. My head and shoulders were drooping. I was exhausted and my muscles ached, not to mention my knee pain from the previous day. Luckily, the brilliant flashing lights of Occento were right up ahead. I was now in the parking lot. I couldn't believe my dazzled eyes. I must have been tired. Occento was even bigger than I had seen on TV. Its dazzling walls went so high up I couldn't see the top. The flashing lights on the word Occento almost blinded me. Feeling utterly dazed, I stepped inside.

It was a shiny, polished building, and everybody was dressed fancy, which made me self-conscious of my own shabby shirt and washed out jeans. In the waiting room, everybody cast appraising, disdainful looks at my clothes, wondering what someone like me was doing in here. My cheeks flushed red with embarrassment. Finally, when my name was called last, I stood up. This was it. My dream. I was getting to sing on Occento!

As I walked up the stage, I felt as nervous as ever. Each nerve in me was tingling so electrifyingly, that I couldn't feel my feet. I was suddenly conscious of a hangnail and a loose thread on my jeans that I had never noticed before.

Finally, I took a deep breath and just like that, I was singing. In Occento, if the judges like your piece, then they hold up a sign. I was last, and the highest scoring contestant had three signs up. The average rest had twos and some ones. If I got a four …

But there was no time to think about that now, while I was going to sing. My body began to relax, and just like that, I was singing with Mama. Somehow, as I was singing, I felt her, her presence with me, singing the song. The first judge put up her sign.

I willed myself to keep going. I sang with all my heart, letting my struggles and failures pour out through my music. I forgot about everything, everyone, until it was just the music, Mama and me. The second judge put up her sign.

Sometime later, while I was singing, I heard sirens. A police car sped up. The doors of Occento open, and in came Baba. When he looked up at me, he froze. My heart seemed to drop down to my stomach. But I carried on, never taking my eyes off Baba. It was a father-daughter staring contest. Sensing that I'd recovered from a great shock, and managed to sing well, the third judge put up her sign. Baba didn't stop me. He let me carry on, closing his eyes and listening. He seemed lost.

I was starting to worry when I neared the end of the song. The fourth judge had still not put up her sign. Ignoring this, I sang the last note of my song, a fifteen-second-high note. Everybody looked astounded. The fourth judge stared at me, right in the eye, then without a word, she lifted the sign.

I couldn't find the words to say. I collapsed onto my knees, holding my hands out and watching the gold glitter streamers swirl into my outstretched arm. I then realized that I was crying.

"Mama." I croaked. "I knew you were with me."

Then Baba ran onstage.

"Oh Anisha," he said, hugging me tightly. We hugged each other and cried and cried.

"I'm sorry Baba." I apologized thickly through my tears.

He only let go of me when the judges came to give us the check enough to make us rich, and details for the new mansion, which was in the same neighborhood!

But as happy as I was, a thousand questions were swirling in my head like the snow that fell on the ground a year ago, during storm Maya.

"How did you know that I was here?"

"I woke up at six and then went to check on you. You weren't in your bedroom. You weren't in the bathroom. You weren't in the kitchen. I went into the savings closet to see if you might be there, and saw the chest lying open. Once I saw that sixty dollars were gone, that thought lingered at the back of my head, but I didn't pursue it. Now I was seriously getting scared. I called the police, and we patrolled the streets. We passed by a tree with straggly dead vines and leaves hanging from it, and a paper stuck to it looked familiar. I looked closer, and it was a flyer for Occento. All at once everything came together. I knew where you were." He hugged me again. "I was so worried."

"Baba?"

"Yes?"

"Why don't you like me singing?"

"Oh Anisha." His eyes had filled again. "I don't dislike your singing. I adore it. But—" he heaved a sigh, "After Mama passed, I was devastated. I was grieving, and I thought, if I shut down all memories of her, then maybe I would be happy again. Or maybe she would come back. But now, thanks to you, I realize that she was here all along, in you, when you sing. And I—" his voice cracked. "—I just shut your dream, Saadia's dream."

"Oh Baba." I felt terrible for him. I think the only person that may have loved Mama more than me is Baba and now she is no more.

Baba suddenly smiled. "But you won! All our dreams came true! We can afford good things now, we can sing all we want, and there will be no Madam Atoosa to complain!"

As we walked home, arm in arm and pointing out the rainbows and cupcakes of Kari's egg incident on the sidewalk, I was smiling the biggest I had ever smiled. Oh yes, I had accomplished my dream. I realized that Mama was gone forever, but that there still was a part of her inside me. We can live a better life. This wasn't the end of singing for me. It had only just begun.

THE END

Pacing

Reagan Ricker worked with mentor, Tasslyn Magnusson, in a revision focused on pacing in Reagan's poem, *Dear Sarah.*

Dear Reader,

Did you know poets think about pacing? **Pacing** is as important in a poem as it is in prose. How does the poet unfold the sequence of events for a reader to build to a satisfying conclusion? Just like the end of a good book, the end of a good poem should make you sit back and say, "Ah! Wow!"

When Reagan and I talked about her poem "Dear Sarah," I explained how active language is an integral part of what moves a reader through a poem. Reagan had terrific uses of alliteration and onomatopoeia throughout her poem. I loved the line, "soft shhh of a soda pop can." In her revision, Reagan built on this foundation to tighten her very honest story about friendship.

We started by thinking about how the colors of the rainbow might represent different challenges in the friendship. I suggested an outline. When I'm thinking about questions like these, I will make an outline. Nothing fancy—just "stanza one is about the girls meeting; stanza two is about the girls become best friends; stanza three is about a fight." You have to write this outline without looking at the poem. Next, compare it to your stanzas. Do things match up?

Because Reagan uses a cool extended metaphor, I encouraged

her to really think through her word choice. Poetry is language and your words should both sound and behave in unexpected—sometimes pleasing, sometimes not—ways. Speaking of not pleasant ways, a great example is when Reagan writes about yellow. Look at all the ways her word choice sounds and feels uncomfortable. "Pucker, twitch, spit, disgust"—these are all good words. How does your mouth feel when you eat lemon juice? Maybe make a list of all the words that also put your mouth in that same shape?

Finally Reagan took advantage of what poets get lots of choice with—line breaks and white space. As part of her revision, I asked Reagan to think about the words and then think about the shapes the words make on the page. What would be the way she could show the good—and the hurt—of this friendship.

If you're writing poetry, maybe you didn't realize some of those things we talk about in regards to prose could apply to poetry. They can. Especially pacing! And they can be really exciting to consider. What kind of stories are you telling in your poems? And don't forget to use your white space. Create a poem that grabs attention on the page and helps the reader feel and see the story you are telling.

Happy Writing!

Tasslyn Magnusson

Tasslyn Magnusson received her MFA in Creative Writing for Children and Young Adults from Hamline University in Saint Paul, MN. Her poems have been published or are forthcoming in Broad River Review, in parentheses, Room Magazine, The Mom Egg Review, The Raw Art Review, and Red Weather Online. She was nominated for a 2018 Pushcart Prize in poetry. Her chapbook, "defining," (dancing girl press) was published in January 2019.

Reagan Ricker

Reagan Ricker is a young teen who enjoys writing poetry and adores English, yet struggles to find time with school. Between her passion with debate, six different sports, and an entrepreneurial business, she is packed with a busy schedule but would never change anything about it. She has been published in the *No Safe Place Anthology,* and won the 2020 *Poetic Power* writing contest as well.

Tasslyn Magnusson: What changed as you revised your poem?

Reagan Ricker: First, I took your advice on reading it aloud. That really helped. When I wanted the reader to close to pause or wait I added a period. Some of the words, I took out the spacing so they would be read faster.

Q: Did you think the poem would change through the revision process?

A: I did. I've always thought that when people judge poems they are looking for the potential in poems, not what it is already.

Q: What advice do you have for Inklings who don't like revision?

A: I think that revision is looking at the work with a new perspective. A teacher told me that as the author, you know what your work is about and you have all the details worked out in your head, and order to make it better, you need to hear it from another person's perspective.

Q: When did you start writing?

A: I think I developed my passion for writing around third grade. Third grade was my chance where I could write and that it evolved as I grew up.

Q: What's the last book you read?

A: *Germs, Guns, and Steel.*

Q: What is a book that you think every writer should read?

A: I can't think of a title off the top of my head but any book that has a different perspective or a different way of writing is important. Every writer should allow themselves a chance to read a different style from them, just to involve more variety in their writing. Basing some of your poetry on real life experiences really helps, and you can certainly add in creative liberty to that.

Q: How do you come up with ideas for poems?

A: I have a continuous list of ideas that I save for poems. Anytime I get an idea and can't work on it, I put it there.

If I'm having writer's block and can't find an inspiration for poems at that time, I go online and find a writing prompt. I use that. I'll shift it into my perspective or adapt it for me.

For short stories, I try brainstorming. A general theme helps narrow it. If you are looking at a broad topic its hard to find a place to start.

Dear Sarah

by

Reagan Ricker

once i tasted a rainbow just me, a white backdrop, and shimmers of light that
fell softly on my fingertips i gently lapped up the spilt colors and they crumbled
when I licked them
like sugar

red
it tasted like sweet, crunchy watermelon chunks,
grainy juice dripping down your chin
leaving a sticky trail for your fretful mother to find later
a cold rag rubbing away at your delicate skin
in hopes that you'll be clean
hot, freshly cemented sidewalks awaited the splatter it would leave
red. two girls sitting side by side,
munching on the leftover rinds that held only sour puddles of water
caramel wispy strands of hair dimpled chins patented Mary Janes
small, colorful pinwheels were scattered across the yard
they spun themselves into oblivion

we laughed and it sounded like music.

pink

it took a while to bite through it

but ended up being naively chewing a ball of bubblegum

i stuck a rusty quarter in the slot, waited for *cha-ching* and got to

working my jaws and pearly whites to a perfectly white center

the outside kind of melted down

into small rivers of a sickly sweet flavor that ran in thin streams between my

taste buds and the gap in my front teeth

pink. it ended up being not realizing the world around us, just blowing

bubblegum and forgetting that

it would eventually pop.

orange

bursts of citrus exploded onto my

surprised tongue

like freshly picked clementines in the summer, resting in a woven basket

where the crumpled leaves with their twisted veins would fall softly to the

grass

and fresh sprays of zest would erupt to reveal tangy fruit

the aftertaste is a bit bitter the aftertaste is always a bit bitter

orange.

snack time

in fourth grade wouldn't be complete without crumbling crackers,

the salt falling off

and cold cheese slices on top of them

a girl next to me smiles, and its contagious

yellow

so easily can I discern that it's a bittersweet color

that I nearly want to spit it out onto a paper napkin,

so that the kite shaped design can absorb my disgust instead

it's addicting this yellow. the way it lures you in so easily

only to betray seconds later

my lips pucker up instantly and my eye begins to twitch rapidly. yellow.

your hair, contrasting with your new summer tan

a dotting of freckles across your nose like grains of sugar

brightly colored flip flops

and a conch shell bracelet that adorns your slender wrist

if i look for too long, i may learn to like the new you

just like everyone else

so I turn my gaze

down

green

this may be the only time i wish it was the crunchy asparagus

the wilting broccoli, watery cucumbers, tough zucchini

that my mother is always nagging me to eat

but it tasted kind of artificial, and synthetic

like rice krispies that were dyed green for st. patrick's day

the ones that always left a cardboard aftertaste and a parched tongue

green. hot, sticky grass that scraped and scratched at our bare thighs

two girls giggling and rolling around at the edge of a park.

turns into our past.

talking engulfs our present

before she begins, i know where it's going to end

"you're so overprotective grow up i have other friends

... i think it's best if we go our separate ways"

but which way do i take, when my only way has been with her?

i open my mouth to interrupt,

to whisper sorry

one more time

but end up exhaling and letting go a breath i didn't know i was holding in.

blue

i try convincing myself that it's sweet,

this pastel light that sits in the palm of my hand

but my brow is furrowed and my lips pursed in a tight knot

because reassurance doesn't do much when you know the truth

blue is pungent and funky, a sour item like the wrong type of cheese

blue. murky lakes, and rubber tire swings

that wedge themselves into sweaty legs

shrieks and hollers of excitement, laughter that's free and easy

the soft *shhhh* of a soda pop can opening,

sweet, sickly liquid that washes away guilt

i try convincing myself you forgot to invite me but

it doesn't work.

purple

i was almost sad to taste it, the last of the colors

it's alone now, left behind by all the others

i'm expecting it to be bitter, yet it has a startling flavor of sugar

and warm honey like an overly ripe plum, the pericarp creased,

juices oozing out of the indigo flesh

it dribbles down my chin like the

watermelon we once shared

i laugh a bit, remembering, and it sounds like a broken music note

purple. you and me, something that only exists in old, cracked photos

and false promises

purple. the color of your smile after you finished dancing but also the color of

petty gossip, and whispered secrets. purple.

being left behind on an open road, not knowing which direction it will

take you but only knowing what you will be leaving by doing so

once i tasted a rainbow

it was knowing that not

everything's black and white not everything is gray

it was realizing life is colorfulandconfusing

no matter how you look at it

dear sarah

once i tasted a rainbow

funny thing was, it tasted like you.

Twists and Turns

Audrina Quiroz worked with mentor, Ailynn Knox-Collin,s on a revision focused on twists and turns in Audrina's flash fiction story, *Nine Lives*.

Dear Reader,

Audrina has written a wonderful piece of flash fiction. That is a story told in very few words. In this piece, Audrina tells a story with lots of twists and turns, ending with a big surprise. All in less than 300 words.

In revising this story, we focused on how to make those **twists and turns** more surprising. Surprise endings and twists in the story are what keep readers reading. Readers remember that feeling of being surprised, and it endears them to the story.

First, we looked at each part of the story, from the opening paragraph onwards, and noted what clues were being dropped at each step. Some clues were important, like the casual mention of the shape of the character's birthmark. But Audrina also had to be careful not to

bring too much attention to that same detail. She added other details that were interesting and would lead the reader's mind away from the birthmark, to prepare for big reveal at the end. An example of this is the mysterious text message. Did it have something to do with the outcome or not?

Secondly, we revised some sentences to keep the story closer to the mind of the character. Because this is a very personal story, revision meant rewriting some sentences to make it more personal to the character's thoughts and experiences.

For example, this sentence,
Momentarily confused, I had taken my hands off the steering wheel to check again who it was from.

was revised to,
Confused, I took my hands off the steering wheel to look more closely at the number.

Keeping the sentence in the simple past tense made the action more immediate.

Finally, we looked at the length of sentences. In the action of the accident, Audrina decided to keep the sentences short and sharp, in order to keep the tension up.

Here, the original sentence read like this:
Then all I saw and heard was a flash of light. the screech of brakes, and a dazzling white glow that seemed to be emitting from in me before everything went black.

Audrina adjusted this paragraph to give it more tension:

All I saw was a flash of light. The brakes screeched. Then my eyes ached as I were blinded by a strange white glow. It seemed to be emitting from my wrist.

I hope you try to write flash fiction. It can be a lot of fun. Think about a big twist at the end and then create small turns within the story to lead the reader to the moment of the big surprise.

Keep writing!

Ailynn Knox-Collins

Ailynn Knox-Collins has been a Montessori teacher for many years and loves sharing her love of books and writing with her students. She has an MFA in Writing for Children and Young Adults from Hamline University. She is the author of several books for young and middle grade readers—mainly science fiction and nonfiction stories. When she's not writing, she is working with her five dogs on agility, obedience, and rally competitions. She is excited to mentor with Young Inklings and share her love for writing with young authors everywhere.

Audrina Quiroz

Audrina Quiroz is in the sixth grade at El Cerrito Middle school in Corona, California. She enjoys drawing and running cross-country for her school. She loves reading and you can typically be found with a book or two within arm's reach. Her love of writing was sparked after attending a creative writing class in the summer at her local library.

Ailynn Knox-Collins: When did you start writing?

Audrina Quiroz: Probably around the end of last year. I've always liked writing. Last year, my creative writing teacher made us write mythologies and other stories and that's when I started enjoying writing.

Q: What sort of stories do you write?

A: I usually write short stories, fantasies based on things that happened in my life. I've started writing a book about a boy who runs cross country. He has a guardian angel who runs with him. He has no friends because he's shy. When he finally makes friends, she disappears. I've written about three chapters. I've planned the whole thing out. I have an idea of where I want to end it. I don't outline. I just see where the story takes me.

Q: What do you like to read?

A: I usually read fantasy or mysteries. Sometimes I read sci-fi. For example: *Harry Potter*, *Hunger Games* and Westerfield's *Uglies*, *Pretties*, etc. Scott Westerfield is my favorite author. He describes everything in really great detail, so that I

can see what his world looks like and his stories are interesting. I try to do that in my own stories too. I try to imagine what everything looks like before I write so that I put it all the details in.

Q: How did you come up with the idea for this story?
A: Most of my ideas come from dreams. I'm pretty sure I got this idea from online site that has short stories. The magic birthmark was one of those stories and I thought it would be cool if the birthmark acted as a countdown for someone's life.

I might even try to make this piece into a longer story, now that I have a lot of time on my hands.

Q: Who do you enjoy sharing your stories with?
A: I share them with my mom and sister first because they help me edit and check spelling. I'm a terrible speller. After that, I share them with my friends because they tell me the truth. It can be hard to take sometimes if I like a part that they don't, but mostly I know they're trying to help with my story.

Q: What are you working on now?
A: I'm working on my book. I write before I go to bed. In the morning I check to see if the ideas were delusional, and then work to make it better.

Q: How did revision change your work?
A: Working in revision made the story a lot better to read. It added more detail and it made the story more pleasing to read because it was easier not to give away the ending away in the beginning.

Nine Lives

by

Audrina Quiroz

As I reached for my groceries from the cashier, my sleeve pulled back and revealed my wrist. The cashier's gaze lingered on it and I quickly pulled my sleeve back down to conceal my nine shaped birthmark. I took my groceries, and left before she could ask anything.

I hopped into the car and started driving home when I got a text message. It was so powerful it made my phone vibrate out of the cupholder where it had been sitting peacefully. I stopped at a red light and opened the message.

It was from an unknown number and the only thing it said was a line from my favorite movie, *Instant Revenge.*

"Wait, I thought you were dead!

Yeah, well it didn't stick."

Confused, I took my hands off the steering wheel to look more closely at the number.

All I saw was a flash of light. The brakes screeched. Then my eyes ached as I were blinded by a strange white glow. It seemed to be emitting from my wrist.

They told me I was close to death when I arrived at the hospital. They debated even trying to do anything. My mother, in tears, begged them to do all they could to save her only child. Try they did.

I flat-lined after four hours of intense surgery.

I was lying on the hospital bed as stiff as a board while the doctors discussed who would tell my mother. They started to file out of the room. I don't know if it was the sound of footsteps or of the door closing but as soon as the doctors left everything slammed into focus. The lights were too bright. The ticking of the clock was earsplitting.

I gasped, and the line started moving again.

I had been dead for 18 minutes.

Doctors still can't explain it. I have had many tests. All of my broken bones and internal injuries healed.

Only one thing has changed. No one has noticed but me.

That nine shaped birthmark on my wrist ... It's now an eight.

Character Drives the Story

Dear Reader,

Character drives a story. Think of your favorite books and how their main characters somehow seem real, true, authentic. As the reader, you watch the character experience adventure, make mistakes, make choices—and change in some way. **Character as the driving force of your work** is what Shreya and I explored during her revision of her story *Sarah's Storybook Adventure #1: Lost in Little Red Riding Hood.*

To get Shreya thinking about her main character's development, I asked some questions about Sarah, such as, "What are her deeper qualities? What are her flaws?"

Shreya had already shown readers that Sarah liked books and didn't like to be bored. But I urged Shreya to give her readers more information: is Sarah shy, brave, funny? We talked about this, and Shreya let me know that Sarah is a little bit clumsy and somewhat brave. Aha! We then discussed how Sarah's strengths—and her weaknesses—affect what happens in every scene.

Shreya and I also had a conversation centered on *What Sarah wants*. Main characters in stories want—or yearn for—something, just like real humans do. As you write your own stories, think about the idea of your main character wanting or needing something. Your readers will then root harder for your character. Your readers will get to watch your character try, and sometimes fail, and then try even harder next time. While revising, Shreya also focused on making it clearer to her readers how Sarah changed by the end of the story. As writers, we need to make sure that our main characters aren't static (unchanging).

Although her revision focused on her main character as the driving force of the story, Shreya was also willing to taking a look at her secondary characters too. Her story was filled with magical beings—a crafty wolf, a disguised wizard, and a powerful enchantress. As she revised, Shreya thought about each of these magical beings and how to make them shine even brighter for readers. Shreya added sensory details in some scenes. She also strengthened dialogue between the characters, as needed.

I really enjoyed working with Shreya because she was able to focus on our big-picture character revision while also concentrating on details that would strengthen her story and allow her writing to be more precise. Being open to all levels of revision like this is challenging! As writers, we're always refining our craft, no matter what our age or our level of experience may be. That's part of the magic of writing.

Happy writing—and revising,

Elizabeth Verdick

Elizabeth Verdick is an author of many picture books and nonfiction books for young children. Her picture books include *Peep Leap, Small Walt, Small Walt and Mo the Tow,* and her latest title, *Bike & Trike*. She received her MFA in writing for children and young adults from Hamline University in St. Paul, Minnesota. Elizabeth has also edited many books for young people of all ages, including elementary-age children, middle-graders, and teens.

Shreya Sujit

Shreya will be a fourth grader at Helios School in Sunnyvale, California. She loves to read, draw, and write. Shreya's favorite animal is a horse, and someday she wants one of her own—a dark brown horse with a bronze-colored tail. Shreya especially enjoys creating stories of adventure and magic. She hopes to grow up to be an author, writing books about horses.

Elizabeth Verdick: Your character, Sarah, enters a fairy tale world and experiences a magical adventure. Knowing that Sarah is the driving force of your story, how did you strengthen her character during the revision process?

Shreya Sujit: I think Sarah became more believable and more realistic, since she now has flaws and makes mistakes that push the story along. The flaws make her seem more realistic because in real life no one is perfect, and the story would be boring if things were easy for Sarah all the time. I learned that a believable character has to have strengths and weaknesses, and has to take actions that make the story more interesting.

Q: Revision allows writers to share more details that appeal to the senses (sensory details). What types of sensory details did you add, and what do you think they did for your revised story?

A: I added details about the Enchantress's wand, described how the wolf tries to gain Sarah's trust, and also added more details on the transformation of the wizard. These will hopefully help people picture what's going on in my character's minds.

Q: Sometimes writers are scared to make changes, or resistant to them because the writing process already takes so long. What helped you to stay open and positive about your revisions?

A: I was open to suggestions because I knew that the story would come out even better at the end of the revision. Also, I put a lot of effort into my story. I wanted it to become even better and the only way to do that is to get feedback and make changes.

Q: What ended up being your favorite change you made to your story?

A: My favorite change was how instead of getting the code wrong to unlock the wall, Sarah showed her clumsiness by tripping and hitting some random letters. I like this because it reminds me of my own clumsiness.

Lost in Little Red Riding Hood

by

Shreya Sujit

CHAPTER ONE
The Big Shock

Sarah was bored. It was halfway through summer vacation, and she had nothing to do. Gazing at her bookshelf, Sarah felt a rush of jealousy. If only she could have a grand adventure like all her favorite heroes from these books—but nothing exciting ever seemed to happen to her. Even Little Red Riding Hood had more adventures than she did. Sarah reached for the tattered book of fairy tales and started reading.

Sarah skimmed past multiple fairy tales. Then the pages almost seemed to turn faster, all on their own. They stopped at *Little Red Riding Hood,* which Sarah began to read. Suddenly, she noticed the wolf's mean glare tracking her across the page, making her feel uncomfortable. The wolf carefully observed her with a harsh stare, as if he knew she was there. Could he actually *see* her? No, that was ridiculous.

Sarah decided that this must have been a trick of the light, or maybe she was so eager for adventure that she was imagining things that weren't there. Sometimes, *imagining* seemed to be the only thing Sarah was good at doing. When she reached out to turn the page, her hand suddenly went right through! With the whooshing sound of pages flipping, Sarah was pulled into an imaginary world.

As the book pages swirled all around her, the pictures became more vivid. Sarah's auburn hair whipped across her face, as a whirlwind spun her around, making her dizzy. She squeezed her eyes shut. Maybe she would wake up, safe in bed, with the realization that this was a bad dream. Then the whirlwind stopped, dropping her. With a loud thud, Sarah fell down on her back onto a hard floor.

When she opened her eyes, Sarah got up and found herself facing a door. She recognized it as her bedroom door because of the Harry Potter poster, horse-breeds chart, and dragon stickers. But the door was locked. Sarah turned around and was about to say, "Mom, my bedroom door is locked!" but stopped short when she saw who was in front of her. The mother from Little Red's story. She was making muffins and placing them in a basket.

This lady with short dark hair and bright blue eyes was not her mom—and this was *not* Sarah's house. Feeling awkward and scared, Sarah tried to quietly open the door to escape. But by accident, Sarah banged her elbow against the teakwood, causing the woman to turn.

"Little Red Riding Hood, quit spying," said the dark-haired woman. "Go give these muffins to Grandma, and remember, don't talk to strangers, Little Red. Stay on the main path that takes you straight through the forest to find her house. You can't miss it."

Why on earth was this stranger calling Sarah "Little Red"?

Sarah looked behind her, but no one else was there. Then Sarah

noticed she was wearing a red hooded overall dress over a white shirt. She suddenly realized that *she* was Little Red Riding Hood! Sarah pinched herself to make sure she wasn't dreaming.

"Ouch!" She felt a slight pain in her lower arm. Awestruck, she realized she wasn't dreaming at all.

Wait a minute, what had happened to the storybook Little Red? Hadn't she gotten eaten by the wolf in some variations of the story? What if Sarah got eaten too? Sarah willed herself to calm down. The storybook Little Red had been devoured only because of her small brain. Sarah was clever. She could outwit any wolf—at least she hoped so.

CHAPTER TWO

The Surprise Behind the Wall

As she walked down the dusty path, Sarah had time to scan her surroundings. She spotted hills in the distance, bird nests in trees, and squirrels scurrying around. She could smell the moist grass, and she heard the melodious chirping of birds.

With a swish of his tail, a wolf crept out from behind some pine trees with a sly look on his face. He was obviously attempting a kindly, innocent expression, but all he could manage was a crooked sneer.

"Hello, little girl, where are you going with those muffins?" asked the wolf, licking his lips.

Cleverly, Sarah didn't respond. Knowing that the storybook Little Red Riding Hood had told the wolf everything he needed to know to

trap her, Sarah ignored him. Little Red Riding Hood might have been a blabbermouth, but Sarah definitely wasn't. She continued walking casually down the path.

"*Urgh*! No one ever falls for *that* trick anymore," the wolf muttered as he stalked off.

Sarah stopped when she saw a brick wall right across the path. There was something strange about this brick wall. It *is* strange to have a wall in the middle of a forest, but there was something even more absurd about this one. Each brick had a letter on it. Next to the wall was a piece of paper. Sarah picked it up and read it aloud:

"Shift by 5 and tell me, who am I?

F E B W N I.

No time for games, I need you to think,

unscramble this word and that is your link."

Sarah was puzzled. Wait! She knew codes from stories she'd read. Maybe it was one of the codes where you shift each of the letters by 5! Sarah easily shifted the letters:

F - A

E - Z

B - W

W - R

N - I

I - D

Sarah unscrambled the letters and got WIZARD. Sarah was excited that she'd solved the code. She jumped up and shouted, "Yes!"

Just as she landed, she accidently rammed her elbow against the wall, hitting two letters.

"Ouch," she muttered.

The wall trembled, and then violently EXPLODED.

Sarah ducked. Somehow *she* had triggered the wall. And now it was open for her! *Lucky me*, she thought.

From the rubble of the bricks, emerged . . . a dragon!

CHAPTER THREE
Sarah's Imagination

"ROARRRRRR!"

The dragon had shiny and sleek red scales, orange horns, and gold markings running up its body. It had fierce, copper eyes with pupils that looked like pennies. The dragon was huge, almost twelve times Sarah's own height, and it could easily outrun her. It did look sleepy though, injured on the wing, and probably not ready to fight. However, it might still breathe fire and Sarah didn't think she could do anything about that.

Wait a minute! In all the books Sarah had read where heroes battled dragons, the dragons didn't seem very intelligent, just territorial. Maybe she could fool this particular dragon somehow.

She looked around frantically for something to hide behind, but there wasn't a tree that was thick enough to protect her. Just when Sarah thought she was about to be burnt, an echoing voice in her head, a voice that wasn't her own, cried out: *Imagine your arms are branches!*

Sarah decided to trust the voice. After all, what would be a better option? Nervously, she stood very still with her feet planted and arms raised. She repeated in her head: *I am a tree. I am a tree.* She envisioned a full-leafed

red maple tree, just like the one she loved to climb in her yard.

The dragon looked around with a confused expression on his face. He couldn't seem to see Sarah. So he walked back towards the heaps of crumbled and charred bricks. Then, in a flash of blinding light, the dragon was gone, leaving the wall just as neat as it once had been.

Before, Sarah might have had a huge reaction to such strange events and gotten really confused. But Sarah had seen so many strange things today that, oddly, even *magic powers* didn't seem shocking.

Feeling relieved that the worst was over, Sarah started gently tapping the bricks with the letters W-I-Z-A-R-D. Nervously, Sarah backed up, prepared for the wall to explode. This time, there was no explosion and no dragon. The wall split neatly in half, allowing Sarah to walk through.

Soon Sarah spotted a little cottage in the distance. Was it Grandma's? About one hundred feet from the cottage, Sarah realized a brick wall was being magically built around it. The bricks hovered in the air until they got added to the wall. Brick by brick, the wall grew taller by the moment.

Just as Sarah was about ten feet from the cottage, the final brick fell into place, and the wall was complete. Sarah knocked on the wall. She pushed the wall. She punched the wall, but all that she accomplished was getting a sore fist.

Sarah needed to see over the wall, but the only way to do that was by climbing it. Stumbling a little here, and slipping a little there, she did her best to climb it. She used the uneven edges of the bricks as hand holds, and with some difficulty, she reached the top. There, standing before her, was a wolf.

"Going somewhere?" the wolf inquired.

Scrambling to her feet, Sarah recognized the wolf as the one she had met in the beginning of the book, and he didn't look like he was in a good mood.

Chapter FOUR
The Enchantress

The wolf stood up on the wall and blocked Sarah's way with his furry, muscular body. Sarah jumped down and started to run. But the wolf was too quick for her.

In the blink of an eye, the wolf was right in front of her again.

"Let's stop with all the running, shall we, and let's start the magic battle," sneered the wolf confidently in his deep, gruff voice. Then he shouted, *"Blastio!"*

A blue bolt shot out of his paw and sped towards Sarah. She ducked and the spell hit a tree, causing it to fall.

Sarah ducked and dodged. The wolf followed her every move. Sarah wanted to run away screaming, but the wolf would probably have some magical way of catching up to her.

Desperately, Sarah racked her brain for a solution, but the only thing that flashed through her mind was: *This isn't supposed to happen in the fairy tale!* Just when she thought her life was about to end, Sarah remembered that she had used her imagination earlier, becoming a tree to fool the dragon.

Sarah squeezed her eyes shut and repeated, "Forcefield, forcefield, forcefield."

Maybe she could protect herself this way. She pictured a bright blue bubble surrounding her. Sarah hoped with all her will that a magical ball of protection would envelop her, causing the wolf's bolts to bounce off like harmless foam balls.

When Sarah opened her eyes, she was surprised and relieved to see that she had a blue ball all around her.

Just then, the wolf sent another blast. *"Blastio Empowero!"*

A bright blue bolt shot toward Sarah like a bullet. She squeezed her eyes tightly.

The spell bounced right off the force field. It hit the wolf smack on his nose. The wolf fell backwards.

"Yeoww!" The wolf made an agonized sound that gave Sarah a chill up her spine. *"Yeeowee!"* the wolf cried again. The sound was somewhere between a howl and a yelp.

As he cried, the wolf's hands grew more distinct fingers, but there was still fur on them. His nose turned humanlike. Then, the fur slowly started to dissolve, replaced with dark blue robes that were speckled with stars. His wet canine lips and squinty eyes gradually morphed into a pale face with dazed green eyes, a small goatee, and curly dark hair. His nose slowly shrank and changed color, which Sarah thought was gross. The ears on the top of his head melted away, little by little. In their place was a tall pointed hat with the same pattern as his robes. His paws had disappeared. Where they used to be were black leather boots with bronze buckles. Slowly, his body transformed into that of ...

"A wizard?" Sarah wondered aloud.

"Yes, you are absolutely correct," said an echoing, mysterious voice.

Sarah recognized it as the voice that had cried the words, *Imagine your arms are branches*. Sarah spun around, curious to see where the voice had come from. She finally spotted who it was: an old lady with white hair pulled back into a bun. She had mysterious silver eyes that looked like they had seen it all, and a black cloak and shawl over a black dress that seemed to float around her. The woman sat in a rickety porch chair, slowly rocking back and forth.

Of course, Sarah thought, *she must be the grandma.*

But there was something magical about this grandma, something Sarah couldn't explain.

"Are you a witch?" Sarah asked, unsure.

"Indeed I am," answered the woman, with a wink. "But I prefer the term Enchantress, if you don't mind."

Sarah had so many questions! But all she could say was: "What's going on?"

"Now Sarah," said the strange woman. "Unlike many people, you have the gift of imagination. When you picture things in your mind, they seem so realistic. You imagine that you are feeling, tasting, and smelling something real, when in reality, there is nothing there."

"So what?" said Sarah. "I bet tons of people have imagination. It's nothing special."

"The power of imagination may seem small and unimportant, but it can change the world," the Enchantress informed her. "You will learn more about this power someday, but today is not the day. Now, back to why you are here. I sucked you into this book, hoping that you would exercise your powers of imagination as you traveled through this story."

Sarah didn't know how she should feel about this. Some strange lady knew her name and had sucked her into this book! Part of Sarah felt as if the Enchantress had no right to interfere with her life. But Sarah was also kind of grateful. Without the Enchantress, she would still be bored.

The Enchantress continued. "The tasks I have set for you going forward will help you practice and strengthen your powers. Now, about this young man." The Enchantress gestured toward the wizard. "I had my young friend here, my apprentice, use his magic to place the idea in your brain that you wanted to read this book. You were sucked into the story, and then

led through the woods by the wizard in disguise, without your knowledge of course. Then you were brought to me."

Sarah glanced at the wizard, who was sitting on the grass, counting the blades, muttering random words, and grinning like a maniac.

"Unfortunately, he believed that he alone should have this gift of imagination and tried to prevent you from reaching me. Now, because of his behavior, he must face the consequences."

The Enchantress stuck her hand into her pocket and pulled out a gleaming teakwood wand. Vines curled around its handle, and the head of an owl was carved onto the tip of the wand. The wood grew whiter as it reached the wand's tip, and the wood there was smooth and straightened.

The Enchantress pointed it at the knocked-out wizard and said, "*Telaportatio!*"

The wizard was gone in the blink of an eye.

"Is he dead?" asked Sarah.

"No, I have simply banished him from entering this story," said the Enchantress. "Now Sarah, I have a very straightforward task for you. Go into the cottage and walk through the first door you see. You'll be back in your room, understand?"

Sarah partly felt like she wanted to go home, but she also wanted to stay with the Enchantress and ask questions. Unfortunately, the Enchantress seemed to have made up her mind.

"We will meet again!" said the Enchantress.

In a flash of light, she was gone.

"Wait!" Sarah cried out. She still had so many questions! But the lady had disappeared. Feeling that she'd had enough adventures for one day, Sarah did as she was told.

Swinging open the cottage door, Sarah looked around. There was a

long hallway full of a variety of doors. Some doors were colorful and some were plain, but one stood out to Sarah. She recognized her bedroom door among all the others, with the familiar posters and stickers on it.

She opened that door. Book pages swirled all around her. And just like the Enchantress had said, Sarah found herself back in her room.

She smelled her mom's grilled sandwiches. Sarah could hear her dad building something in the garage, his hammer pounding on wood. Sarah plopped onto her bed. She hugged her horse stuffed animal, feeling glad to be somewhere familiar again.

Now Sarah was definitely not bored. She had experienced the best afternoon of her life. Sarah couldn't wait to have another storybook adventure!

THE END

Character Arc

Dear Reader,

How often do you find yourself reading a story, wondering what will happen next? The complexities of a plot are often the first things you'll recount when telling other people about a new story you've read or seen. The ups and downs get your heart racing as you ride along with the characters through the story. But how often do you recount the moments where the characters in the story underwent a change? Beyond plot, another important aspect to storytelling—the one that creates the characters you fall in love (or hate) with—is the **character arc.**

Pierce had developed an intriguing premise prior to the editing process: The body of a school teacher, assumed to be murdered, goes missing. Our main character, Detective Smellburg, finds himself in an elite private school environment of those destined for great things in life. His background is far from that of the students attending the school, though he can relate to the teachers who work day and night to educate their students. The detective prides himself on catching every last criminal he's ever come across, and is skilled in rooting out motivations of his suspects

through heavy questioning.

But things don't always go as planned. Essentially, an arc is a change from one state to another over the course of the story. In extreme cases, good guys may become evil or bad guys may even save the day. Characters set off on their story, sure of themselves and with their motivations set on the outcome they believe is how the world should be. But by the end, these same characters may have a change of heart, or a realization that they might have been wrong all along. The development of a rich character arc allows the audience to empathize and understand why a character takes his or her actions over the course of a story, and why a character may change their mind.

In Pierce's story, the detective is confident that he'll get to the bottom of the mystery and send a murderer to jail. But by the end, he allows his perpetrator to escape for the first time ever. He discovers the true motive behind the crime, and has a change of heart. Through the editing process, Pierce was able to dive into the backstory of his characters, and bring dialog and motivations to the page that helped us understand the changes the detective as well as the suspects went through as a result of the crime. We can understand why a detective committed to truth and justice found a way to justify hiding the truth.

Happy Writing,

Alex Doherty

Alex Doherty is a writer based in the San Francisco Bay Area and has an MFA in screenwriting. He worked as a Story Assistant for film and TV production in Los Angeles before working as an Assistant Producer in video game development. He's inspired by the creativity of others and enjoys theater, movies, reading and finding time to practice his green thumb when he's not backpacking.

Pierce Wright

Pierce Wright resides in New York City and is a rising eighth grader at The Browning School. An avid reader for many years, Pierce primarily enjoys reading science fiction books, especially multi-part series. In his free time, Pierce enjoys playing with friends, listening to music, riding bike and running cross country.

Alex Doherty: Where did the idea for your story begin?

Pierce Wright: In English class we were asked to write a mystery story. I used some of the teachers and faculty at my school as a starting point for characters in the story.

Q: What did you discover about your character's backstory as you worked on your revision?

A: I discovered as I revised my work that he was more of a lower middle class New Yorker—a juxtaposition with the fancy private school he was investigating.

Q: If another young writer is working on developing backstory for a character, what would you encourage them to try?

A: Try making your characters have some unique things that brings them to life.

Q: Did anything about the revision process surprise you?

A: The revision process was a lot easier than I thought it would be. Writing the original draft was much harder.

Q: What advice do you have for Young Inklings about revision?

A: Revising makes your story better so keep an open mind as you work through the process.

Q: What do you like best about writing?

A: I really like having the control to make the story say and do what I want. Having artistic license to create stories and characters can be really powerful.

Q: What are your favorite books to read?

A: My favorite books are more in the science fiction realm and some of my all-time favorite books include the *Harry Potter* series and the *Gone* series.

Q: Anything else you want to tell Young Inklings?

A: At first writing a story can seem intimidating but once you get into, it can be a lot of fun.

File Number 52: Ms. Passno

by

Pierce Wright

As I approached 52 East 62nd Street in the heart of Manhattan, home of The Browning School, I found myself oddly drawn to the place. I couldn't keep myself from thinking: So here it is; the tony all-boys prep school renowned for minting Ivy Leaguers and captains of industry, a place where teachers make it a career—their life's work—to mold boys into men (or so I've heard). I never thought the likes of me—a scholarship kid from Queens—would walk through its sacred red doors and be ushered into the depths of its hallowed hallways. But here I was, veteran NYPD Detective Henry Smellburg, prepared to find out more about the mystique that is Browning.

Upon arrival, I walked down the eerie hallways that were lined with pictures of former graduates and filled with students and teachers consoling each other. I finally found the office I was looking for—my crime scene—not knowing that something darker than the supposed crime was going to be revealed.

On my way from the precinct to the school, the responding officers and CSI had filled me in on the details of the crime: at approximately 3:30 p.m. a Ms. Marjorie Olney, middle school science teacher, stopped by the

office of a Ms. Danielle Passno, as was her usual routine, but this time it was very different. When she walked in, she found Ms. Passno's mangled body on the floor. Ms. Passno, the admired head of the middle school, was covered in blood with many knife-like wounds. Ms. Olney could be heard shrieking as she ran to the Head of School Dr. John Botti's office and shared the news with him. Dr. Botti called the police but by the time the first officers arrived at the scene, the body had vanished. Without a trace, Ms. Passno was gone. That's where I come in. There is no case I can't crack; there's not a single criminal I've investigated that hasn't been convicted. They are all biding their time at Rikers.

The cops mulling around cleared out as I entered the crime scene; they know I like to review the scene alone. I was told there was a stabbing but, unlike every other murder scene I have witnessed, nothing seemed off. There wasn't even a drop of blood on the carpet. Curious. It didn't even look like a crime had happened in the office other than the mess. There were piles of books thrown to the floor and bins of Legos, apparently leftovers from a school-wide project, were spilled everywhere which made me wonder if there had been a struggle. I glanced over the evidence that CSI had collected at this point to see if there were any immediate clues that might point me in the direction of the killer. Here's what jumped out at me: an email from an English teacher named Ms. Lydon Vonnegut that was suspiciously in Ms. Passno's trash folder after the time of death and a knife with a red blood-like substance on it that would be tested and dusted for fingerprints. There was a Browning pep rally towel that might have been used to wipe the fingerprints and a few Ricola wrappers in the trash can. For a school with such a prestigious reputation, something seemed off—way off. I needed to find out more information about the towel and more about that email.

After a restless night thinking about the case and pondering a lot of scenarios about what could've happened, I arrived at the school building early

to start conducting interviews as soon as teachers arrived. My first person of interest was Ms. Vonnegut, who'd written the email we found in Ms. Passno's trash folder. When I strolled into her classroom I was greeted by a kind woman with an easy smile who was wearing a floral blue dress and heels. There were photos of family in frames on her desk and college diplomas on the wall. She didn't look like a likely suspect but one thing I've learned from the past three decades on the job is that murderers come in all shapes and sizes.

I said, "Hello, Lydon Vonnegut? I am Detective Smellburg. I was hoping that I could take a few minutes of your time to talk about Ms. Passno and her murder."

Not giving her a second to duck my questions, I launched into my interview. "Was there anything unusual about Ms. Passno's behavior or mood over the past few weeks or days?"

"Nothing really that I noticed. She was a little distracted but she's a busy lady so that's not unusual. She was fighting off a cold, but I think we all are; it's that time of year."

"Do you have any connections with Ms. Passno outside of work?" I wondered if she and Ms. Passno might have had a disagreement outside of Browning.

"No," she replied. "I only know her as the head of the middle school."

I wanted to better understand her email to Ms. Passno so I inquired, "What did you mean in that email that was in Ms. Passno's office? That email said that you were going to involve Ms. Passno in something."

"It was about a teacher supposedly quitting their job," she said as she shrugged her shoulders. "It doesn't have any connection to the murder."

I wondered why she would add that last bit.

"One more thing, why would the email you sent her be moved in Ms. Passno's trash folder after she died?"

Ms. Vonnegut looked at the floor and twisted her dress in her hand before she answered, "How would I know?"

"All right," I said as I wondered why she was being so evasive. "Thank you for your time, Ms. Vonnegut. I will be in touch if I have any follow-up questions."

"Anytime," she said. "Glad to help out."

She didn't seem to have a motive, but some of her responses raised the hair on the back of my neck. I couldn't completely rule her out. I needed more information about who might have access to Ms. Passno's office, who might have wanted to see her dead, and who may have taken her body so I set out to talk with more of the teachers.

I went to the classroom that was directly next to Ms. Passno's office. A classroom belonging to a Mr. Daniel Ragsdale, a fifth grade teacher. Since his room is so close to Ms. Passno's I figured he might've been a witness. I casually walked up to Mr. Ragsdale's room and came across a man in a blue and white checkered button down shirt with khakis immersed in whatever he was doing on his laptop. I entered the classroom, introduced myself and although he was grumpy about being interrupted agreed to talk with me.

"Mr. Ragsdale, how long have you worked here at Browning?" I asked.

"Geez, let's see, I can't believe it but I've worked here for 22 years—my whole career," he said.

"Then you've probably seen a lot of teachers and administrators come and go over the years?"

"No, not really," he said. "No one ever leaves here, just the students when they graduate, but not the teachers." I made note of that last bit on my notepad.

"I was wondering, Mr. Ragsdale, did you see anything happen around the time of the murder?"

"Hmmm. I heard it was sometime after school. Let me think. Yes, I saw a tall person, I think a man, walking towards Ms. Passno's office around then."

"Do you know anyone who would be that height?"

"Well, there is only one person in the building around that height. Sam Permutt. Sam is the director of student life and coach for the basketball team. Sam works very closely with Danielle—he is always in and out of her office."

"Was there anything unusual about seeing him yesterday?"

"The only thing that would be strange is that the person I saw was in clothes like I'm wearing and Mr. Permutt is always in sweats after school due to basketball practice."

"Would Mr. Permutt have anything to gain from Ms. Passno's death?"

"He would have a lot to gain from Ms. Passno's death. If she weren't here, he'd become the head of the middle school."

Interesting, I thought to myself as I wondered if the basketball team uses pep rally towels. "Last question. Is the head of the middle school a good job?"

"Well, it pays nicely," he replied.

Hmmm, I thought usually if the pay is the best thing about a job then there are probably a lot of drawbacks. I asked, "What's the worst thing about being head of the middle school?"

"Well, that'd be hard for me to say," said Mr. Ragsdale hesitating. "You'd have to ask Danielle... uh, I mean someone who's had the job."

"Thank you for your time, Mr. Ragsdale. If you think of anything else that might be helpful to the investigation, anything at all, give me a call," I said as I slipped my card across his desk.

"Sure thing, Detective Smellburg."

I set out to find Mr. Permutt as he was now my lead suspect in the case. It seemed like the evidence pointed to him since he had the means, motive and

opportunity: he was seen by her office after school, he had access to the towel and, most importantly, he had something to gain. I set out to find my prime suspect but worried he could be anywhere in the school or could even have already left the building. As luck would have it, he was walking up the stairs and went into his office. Perfect timing.

"Why hello, Mr. Permutt," I said.

"Uhh, who are you?" Mr. Permutt said frantically, even though he had nothing to be afraid of because he was a tall, young, fit man who could probably beat me in a fight, even in his blue button down shirt, tie and khakis. I wondered if he was nervous because I caught him off guard or because he was hiding something. I certainly hoped he wouldn't take off in a sprint because I did not relish the idea of trying to tackle this guy.

"I am detective Henry Smellburg from the NYPD and I wanted to ask you a few questions regarding the murder of Ms. Passno."

"All right then, it couldn't possibly be me."

"Why not?" I asked, thinking to myself that only the guilty ones respond that way.

"You see I was coaching the 7th and 8th grade basketball team until 5:30 p.m. then I had to change into my normal work clothes for dinner, that's why I was not in my usual Browning sweats," he said, adding that last bit as if he could read my mind wondering why he had changed clothes.

"Where and with whom were you having dinner last night?"

"I don't really see why that's relevant, Detective, but I was dining with a lady friend of mine," he replied. "It was our third date so I took her to my favorite restaurant called Paola's." I took note of the name so I could confirm his story later.

"How long have you known Ms. Passno, Mr. Permutt?" I asked.

"She hired me right out of grad school. That was six years ago now. Times flies." he responded.

"In those six years, have you ever had a disagreement with Ms. Passno?"

"Well, I mean, sure, we didn't always see eye-to-eye," he said as he fidgeted with his keys. "But, I mean do you always see eye-to-eye with your colleagues?"

Choosing to consider that a rhetorical question, I continued my interrogation. "Can you explain the team's pep rally towel in Ms. Passno's office?"

"Ah, yes," he said confidently. "I forgot the towel at a basketball game and a student brought it back. They left it with Danielle and she told me it was in her office earlier that day. I went to pick it up around 3:30 p.m. before practice, but her door was locked."

"Interesting. I'll be in touch, Mr. Permutt."

I wasn't buying Mr. Permutt's alibi, especially since Mr. Ragsdale said that Mr. Permutt had something to gain. He certainly had a motive, but I needed more evidence to build my case.

I went back to Ms. Passno's office to review the crime scene to see if CSI had missed anything that might help me. I also wanted to review the file that came in overnight to see if I overlooked anything. A few things piqued my interest.

I noticed a torn piece of paper which was titled "Employee Contract Quitting Regulations." I didn't know what it was but it stated: "All employees that leave the school for unnatural reasons such as quitting before retirement will have to hand over everything they earned while working at this school."

I also found a note from Ms. Vonnegut saying that she stopped by to talk with Dr. Botti but his door was locked. She had presumed he was in a meeting. There were also more of the same cough drops in the office, this time with a CVS receipt. I noticed it had a purchase date and time of 1/18/20 at 9:45 a.m. This meant that whoever had purchased these had visited the crime

scene after the murder, since the murder happened on 1/17/20. I also took down the credit card number on the receipt to see if we could track the owner of the number.

Suddenly, I remembered all of the wrappers in the trash can from before! I figured the culprit would be on their way to CVS soon to get more cough drops. My plan was to go to CVS at the same time the next day and see if anyone would come to buy cough drops.

The stakeout, which was just me leaning against a wall watching people come in and out, started off very boring but then, the unexpected happened. I saw someone enter the store who was way over dressed for the weather. The oversized coat, sunglasses and scarf wrapped around the head were a dead giveaway that whoever this was didn't want anyone recognizing them.

I followed the person and watched as they headed to the cough drop section. I got behind her in line and watched her buy some cough drops and I got the credit card number which happened to be the same as on the receipt I found at the school. Before my brain could process all this, the person had already walked out of the store and onto the busy Manhattan sidewalk. Not sure which way to go, I suddenly caught a glimpse of the scarf and chased after my mystery person.

"NYPD," I said as I showed my badge. "I need to see your ID"

"Excuse me?" the person replied. "What's this about?"

"I'm the one who will be asking the questions," I responded. "Now, show me your ID"

The ID said "Danielle Passno" in bold letters. How could this be? Was this the murderer? I took the mystery suspect back to the police station where I checked her fingerprints and ran them through the system. It appeared to actually be Ms. Passno.

Figuring that she'd talk more freely with me if my interview felt less official I led her out of the station and into an alleyway to question her.

"So let's cut to the chase, Ms. Passno," I said fiercely. "Why did you fake your death?"

"It's a long story." She said nervously as she glanced around the room. "It's a really long story"

I cut her off. "I want the full story. Now," I demanded, "Start to finish."

"It all started when I was getting tired of being head of middle school," Ms. Passno started, then hesitated.

"Go on..."

"I've been at Browning since I was 22 years old—I started teaching there because I love watching the boys' brains learn and absorb information. Teaching is a calling. But over the years I was promoted so many times and finally a few years ago became head of the middle school. But it's a boring desk job. No more teaching. Just endless paperwork and unhappy parents to deal with."

As she spoke it made me think about what would happen if I was the chief and only did paperwork.

Ms. Passno continued, "So I went to the headmaster Dr. Botti to talk about my options of leaving Browning and he showed me the part of the contract where it says 'All employees that leave the school for unnatural reasons such as quitting before retirement will have to hand over everything they earned.' I was devastated. The way Browning pays its employees is unusual you see. They give you a stipend to live off of, but you get your full pay after being here for 30 years. Since I have been here for so long I am owed a hefty amount and I can't afford to lose all the money I earned because what would I do then?"

"I see," I said as I tried to process this strange payment structure. "And around what time did you meet with Dr. Botti? And how does your dying help your situation?"

"That was around 3:30 p.m."

This explained why the door was locked when Mr. Permutt went to get his pep rally towel, and was matching up with my time line.

"Dr. Botti was sympathetic with me and thought that if someone wanted to leave, they should be able to without giving up all their money, but the school's Board of Directors didn't want good teachers to ever leave so we devised a plan to fake my death. He got Ms. Vonnegut, the English teacher, to make some fake wounds to stage my death and then sneak me out of the building. But he had to tell her which ways to take me to not be seen and then we planted the letter in my office to throw people off. Because death is considered natural, I would keep my money as it would be sent to my family, which I would then retrieve. Faking my death at school meant no one would look for me at home. That's my story."

"All right," I said. "And if the people who own the school know you are alive and want to quit, they'll take everything?"

"Yes, that's right," replied Ms. Passno with a tone in her voice that sounded like she was worried about losing everything.

I thought about how I would feel if I were stuck in a boring desk job pushing paper or about to lose all the income I had earned over the years. This situation didn't feel right.

"It's a weird turn of events, but your secret is safe with me. No one has to know you faked your death. Not even the police. And, by the way, I am going to look into the school's payment policy."

"Thank you so much, Detective Smellburg," Ms. Passno exclaimed as she bear-hugged me. "Will you be at risk of losing your job?"

I replied, "My job is to solve mysteries, not follow school rules."

Rhythm

Ynez Foxe-Robertson worked with mentor, Desiree Middleton, to accentuate rhythm, and the way rhythm affects your reading experience of this vibrant poem, *Stems and Leaves.*

Dear Reader,

Ynez focused on editing her poem *Stems and Leaves* from the perspective of **rhythm**. Because Ynez focused on anthropomorphizing plants and insects, she could see them as having a rhythm. Rhythm in poetry means many different things like varying sentence structure.

For Ynez, since she is an artist, I had her think about her poem from an artistic perspective. Every piece of art has a rhythm to it. There are parts of the art piece that draw your eye in slowly, and other parts that ask you to zip your eyes along to capture all that occurs within the art piece. Your poem should be like that artwork. There should be moments that make the reader linger, and moments that make the reader zip along.

As you edit your own poem, think about seeing it as a piece of art. Where do you want the reader to linger? What words can you use to convey a slowage of time, or a speeding up of time?

Happy writing,
Desiree Middleton

Desiree Middleton is an award-winning screenwriter who loves creating imaginative worlds and characters to fill them. She is addicted to Twinkies and resides in Los Angeles.

Ynez Foxe-Robertson

Ynez Foxe-Robertson is a rising sixth grader who loves octopi and glitter. She enjoys learning about the Revolutionary War and loves to read. Her dream is to become a famous fashion designer but also enjoys creative writing. She loves pink and quite enjoys writing poems and limericks. She wrote the poem because she has a mom who enjoys gardening and had many visions.

Desiree Middleton: What was revision like for you?

Ynez Foxe-Robertson: It was good. It does take some work and you have to think hard. My mentor gave me good advice, and my poem changed for the better.

Q: What advice would you give to the other Inklings who don't like revisions?

A: I never had to edit a creative piece before. But the rhyme of the poem needs to be smooth with pizzazz. Movement like the wind or ocean.

Q: When did you begin writing?

A: Because I was applying to an art school I wanted to get into their writing program. I take joy in writing.

Q: What poems or stories do you think you'll work on next?

A: I think I'll work on a short story for another Young Inklings contest.

Stems and Leaves

by

Ynez Foxe-Robertson

The loving snow peas intertwine
As the sunflower sticks out her
tongue in disapproval.

The dandelions giggle
As they blow into the wind.

The graceful tigerlily dances in the sun,
hoping to be noticed.

The bullying pitcher plant urges the fly to take a
peek into its bowlish mouth
as the fly turns its back.

Mother tree has her back turned
when little sapling smiles and sticks out his root,
attempting to trip other plants.

The rosebush blushes
when the Indian paintbrush kisses her hand.

The calla lily politely curtsies in her lush green evening gown.
As the venus flytrap snaps his jaws
annoyingly to the snapdragon.

Then the cherry blossom starts to sing then
the garden goes quiet.

Building Toward a Climax

Steven Cavros worked with mentor, Naomi Kinsman, on a revision focused on building toward the discovery at the climax in Steven's story, *The Old Man*.

Dear Reader,

Steven's lyrical story, *The Old Man*, invites a reader to stop, to savor, and to think. At the climax of his story, we witness his character make a life-changing discovery. Steven chose to keep that discovery a bit mysterious—after all, it's one of those moments when a person sees what's around him and realizes ... *there's more to life than I fully notice in my day-to-day experience.* That's the kind of discovery that no one can really explain. It needs to be experienced to be understood.

So, as we revised Steven's story, we decided to focus on tucking tiny moments throughout the story, like pearls on a string, to **build to the climax**. Those moments would draw the reader close to Steven's character, making it more possible for them to feel his journey along with him. That way, when we reached the climax, we'd be ready for that moment of epiphany along with his character.

First, we looked through the story to see what hints Steven had

already planted. What, generally, was the awakening all about? We noticed there were a number of times in the story where Steven mentioned the character's fears. We also saw that his character seemed to hesitate before making choices, and often let others choose his next steps for him. We decided that the journey might be about fear and courage and trust.

So, our next step was to find opportunities in the story to plant small moments of growth. Where might Steven's character have the opportunity to face his fears along the journey? Where might he have tiny wins, and where might he have set-backs?

Finally, once we found those opportunities, Steven spent time working on those scenes. While he didn't make major changes, he added a sentence or two here and there, and those tiny, focused additions became like little arrows for the reader. *Notice this*, they say. *And this.*

If you'd like to try a revision that builds to the climax, try the steps Steven used. Before starting on the first step, give yourself some time away from your piece. You'll need a little perspective to clearly see the opportunities you've planted for yourself. A friend is also helpful, someone who can read your story and tell you the moments that stand out to them. One way to clear your mind and prepare yourself is to read a compelling story... like, say, *The Old Man* by Steven Cavros!

Happy Reading and Revising,

Naomi Kinsman

Naomi Kinsman is the author of the *From Sadie's Sketchbook* series and the founder of Society of Young Inklings. She takes great joy in celebrating and sharing the incredible voices of youth authors, through projects like the *Inklings Book*.

Steven Cavros

Steven Cavros is a rising fourth grader living in south Florida. Besides writing, he also enjoys songwriting, sketching, painting, and playing the piano. He lives with his pet cat, hermit crab, and fish. Oh, and his mom and dad, too. When he grows up, he aspires to be an author and songwriter.

Naomi Kinsman: How do you set up for a writing session?

Steven Cavros: So usually I'm pretty loose about where I write, just anywhere that suits me. Sometimes I'm not having a day that's great for creativity, but I'm not often faced with this problem. I don't have any specific set-up but usually I'll write almost anywhere when ideas come to me.

Q: Why do you enjoy writing?

A: Well, life can be hard-pressed, that's the best way to say it. Writing is a place to escape to, for me. In writing, it is really my own world where I can, for the most part, control everything. I can make anything happen in my story. Pretty much whatever I can imagine, I can make real in my story.

Q: How do you come up with ideas for your stories?

A: The best way to phrase it is probably that ideas come to me at the worst and most unexpected times, which often means 1:00 in the morning. Well, that might be a bit of an exaggeration, but that gets the point across. Ideas just come and I write them down on little slips of paper. Most of these ideas, nothing ever comes of them, but a few of them actually become something.

Q: How did it feel to revise your story with an editor?

A: Let's put it this way. It was a struggle, but I came through. As most writers are, I was attached to my work, but I came through in the end (thanks to my wonderful editor). For the most part, I think my edits improved the story.

Q: You focused on building your plot to the climax in your revision. What kinds of changes did you make?

A: I suppose it was revising the story, looking for places that moved the story forward. There are these little bits that are hidden throughout the book that are the heart of the story, and these little bits slowly work their way up to the climax. The key to working up to the climax was finding these little places that were already there, and I built on each of these little scenes.

Q: What advice might you give to other writers who are ready to revise a story?

A: I suppose the best thing you can do is to approach it with an open mind. Look hard and see how your edits improved the story. Even if you don't see it at first.

Q: Are you working on a new story now?

A: I'm kind of always working on a story. Usually it's just in my head. Many of my stories are in my head, and only about 1% of these stories actually make it onto paper. But I'm kind of always working on a story in my head. And yeah, I am working on a story right now. Lots of them, in fact.

The Old Man

by

Steven Cavros

The cement was painted a dull, sickening shade of green, tinged with brown. All the houses were lined up in single file. Many of the windows were blackened, and the door hinges were rusted, but it was the place Amo`n called home. A funny word, home was. Home was the place where his mother was, and his infant brother, To`l. His father had been killed in the war, and his younger sister died of sickness. His elder brother had been sent to fight in the war. And so now he called this place home. As in his mind he pondered all he had been through, he nearly strode right past door number 1857. Only one hinge held the door in place—the others had all rusted. There was no formal door-handle. It was customary where he once lived to have no formal handle, no lock. The first time had he seen a handle or lock was at the courthouse, where his family had been assigned number 1857 Dalter Street, in this depressed slum.

Along the weathered pavement came an old man in a yellow rain slicker and a pair of blue boots. He had a long gray beard, wild and unkempt. His hood was cast aside, revealing long gray hair, fraying at the edges. But despite all the old-ness about him, for Amo`n could find no better word to

describe him, the strange old man's eyes had a vivid look. They were pale blue—the blue of rain and wind, fire and sea—and his gaze was piercing. As quickly as he had appeared, the old man was gone.

And there Amo`n stood, awed and dumbfounded. He watched the spot where the old man had rounded the curb and vanished until Amo'n became aware of himself. It was a very long while before he did so.

At last he entered his home, but the main room was deserted. The main room was where they kept the small table that they had been allowed to bring from their old place, and it was where they dined.

Amo`n peeked into his, his mother's, and To`l's bedroom. There, his mother hunched over a simple foil-oven she had thrown together back in their old place. The oven was one of those few possessions they had been allowed to bring to their new home.

That evening they ate beans out of a can and some cheap canned sardines, but Amo`n had quite lost his appetite. All that night he pondered the old man. The old man was very not-ordinary, rather unusual in that depressed slum, which aroused many questions in Amo`n. Who was the old man, and where had he come from? The next morning Amo`n's thoughts dwelled on the old man, and all through that day and the next. Time passed slowly. At last, on the fifth day, something happened.

After he and his family had said their morning prayers, Amo`n dunked himself in a bucket of warm water that they stowed in the alley (that was also where they had their pit toilet). It was custom to bathe every morning in his religion, to have a fresh start. Amo'n went out on the curb to await the bus. In his pack he had stowed all he would need that day: Do`ldi`l, his old stuffed animal from his last place—once his elder brother's that he later inherited, his lunch—a can of cold, hard Machu` beans, his few valuables, and the shaker gourd he'd made out of a coconut.

As he did most days, he would board the bus, which would take him to Beech Road. There, he would hitch a ride to the big city, where he would sit on the curb and wave a sign. Later, he would hitch another ride to the Kendl Jair forest preserve, just outside the city, where he could catch lizards and bugs with his hands. He had always loved nature ever since he was young. Back in his old home. That evening he would come home, do his evening chores, say his evening prayers, take his evening barrel-bath, and sleep in a thatched cot he himself had crafted, on the hard, bare floor.

Amo`n settled down on the bench—which was missing a leg and worn where paint had flecked off—and he began to ponder the strange old man. Then, along came a certain man of great age, who Amo`n recognized indeed, with pale blue eyes, and long wisps of grey hair that hung down his waist. Again, he wore a yellow rain slicker and a pair of blue boots. His beard was wild and tangled. The old man walked over to the old bus bench and took a seat beside Amo`n. He did not speak a single word for a long while.

Many times, Amo`n attempted to speak to the old man, but he could not bring himself to do so for a long while.

At last Amo`n managed to inquire, "Sir, are you umm... waiting for the morning bus?"

"Be the answer no or yes, I am here. Be it yes or no, am I not here?" replied the old man.

"But umm... well, this is the bus stop," said Amo`n.

"It is a bench, and I am here, and you are here, but it matters naught why we meet—why I wait. I am here." The old man said no more, and Amo`n said no more.

The morning bus came along, though Amo`n did not feel like boarding it. What would do him best was a fine walk in Kendl Jair, but he had to put his family's needs before his own. Even so, he rarely collected a penny

wandering the streets. About six hours later, Amo`n had collected about seven cents, along with many dark glances and dirty looks. He was quite worn out. It was the warm season, and he was very thirsty. He hitched a hike to Kendl Jair, where they had public drinking fountains and other facilities.

It was almost dark by the time Amo`n reached Kendl Jair, where he hiked two trails and filled his old Machu` bean can with water, for he had no bottle. From the fountains he hiked the short trail that led from the water fountains to the exit. An old, rusted bench sat beneath the "grey pavilion" as Amo`n called it, right by the exit. Amo`n was quite weary, but it was getting dark and he needed to be home soon. A few minutes later he passed through the grey pavilion, and he considered resting on the bench, but he decided not to.

Then, upon the bench he spotted the old man again, with his long gray hair and beard. He still wore his yellow coat and blue boots. He had an odd air about him as he sat on the bench humming softly to himself. Amo'n attempted to pass the old man casually, but he was barely a few feet from the pavilion when his curiosity overcame him. He hurried back, and as he entered, the old man looked up.

"So, you could not restrain yourself any longer," the old man said, more a statement than a question. He seemed in part to be speaking to himself. "Ah, indeed, it is well you have come," said the old man. "I can bestow upon you a great wealth, one that would bring you and your family out of poverty, out of all of your depression."

"Could you lead me to a treasure so grand?" asked Amo`n.

"Indeed, I can lead you to a great treasure, but there is more to all than what meets the eye. Yes, it is costly, a wealth so great, and you must trek miles along barren pathways. It is there you will gain something grand."

"What may be the costs of which you speak?" inquired Amo`n, but he was far too excited to really comprehend what the old man was saying.

"Some costs, which I will not name," said the old man simply. "Now we shall be off."

And quite promptly, with surprising haste for a man of his great age, the old man leapt to his feet, and dashed off into the trees. Amo`n raced after him.

The old man led Amo'n through the woods of Kendl Jair, and out through the exit. Then they cut across the east half of the city, through a cluster of small, slum-like, depressed neighborhoods. At last it became too dark to continue, and Amo`n knew naught where he was heading. They were also both very weary, and Amo`n began to see some of the "unnamed costs" the old man had spoken of. They slept out in the alley of a very poor neighborhood, almost as poor as Amo`n's neighborhood. The old man produced some matches from his pocket and a flashlight, for it seemed he had been expecting this strange meeting and unexpected journey. The old man also had two small cans of beans and chicken and rice, stowed in the pockets of his old yellow raincoat. He gave can of beans to Amo`n, and took one for himself. Then, he busied himself with preparing their meal. It was a slow process, but food of any sort felt good now, especially warm food. Amo'n had not had warm food since yesterday's breakfast. He always ate cold lunch, and often cold dinner. The two spoke little as they ate, and then rested, and eventually Amo`n drifted off into an uneasy sleep. Many times during the night, he was awoken by strange noises. At one point he heard shouting in a house nearby and saw two figures dashing down the street.

The morning came as a relief. After eating a breakfast of (warm) Machu` beans, the two travelers set off again. Slowly the slum-ish side of the city faded into barren wasteland, where only grass and small shrubs grew. Amo`n and the old man walked in single file, along paths carved into hillsides that often led to sheer drops. Each time they came to a dead end, they had to

select a new path—long and grueling labor. Once, they came to a point where the path they were following strayed to their left and led to a rather nasty drop. They had to walk back along that path for what seemed quite a while, though it was only twenty minutes, before they found a new path. This new path led to a fork in the road, which, in Amo`n's situation was far worse than the roads that led to drops or dead ends.

Now he had to choose one path, and, really choosing was not Amo`n's strong point. Plus, either of these paths could lead far astray, and there might not be another path for miles around.

But, the man left it to Amo`n to choose the path. After about half an hour—it seemed the longest half hour of Amo`n's life—he chose the left path. Previously, Amo`n had been attempting to keep track of each step the old man took. He gave up at three thousand, five hundred and sixty- seven. Once he stopped counting, each moment seemed to drag by. Slowly time passed, until at last Amo`n and the old man stopped to rest and eat their cold lunch. Again, the old man did not fail to produce lunch provisions from deep inside his yellow rain slicker's pockets.

It was some time after lunch when Amo'n and the old man set off again. The land was barren and forlorn. Even the air current stood still, it seemed. Time itself seemed to have ceased.

Little occurred that day. Little, that was, until darkness settled upon the land. Amo`n's legs ached, and he wished to rest. However, the old man said they must continue, for they were currently too exposed.

"The cover of the trees is near" said he.

Suddenly Amo`n became even more aware of the costs of their journey. Previously, his excitement to claim the "great wealth" of which the old man spoke had driven all other thoughts away. Now his exhaustion and worries returned and burdened him greatly.

Just then he heard a strange noise. It sounded almost like a whisper in the dark, but he could not understand what the voice had said. The words repeated, becoming clearer. And Amo'n cringed when he heard the words. Never again in his life did he dare utter what he heard—the voice spoke of treachery and torment, of darkness and depression. Amo'n's spirits were dampened greatly, and as he walked the voice grew clearer. At last the old man announced they would shortly be stopping to rest for the night. And then, there loomed before Amo'n great shapes. The voice drew near, and it now issued from all around him. He could now barely see the old man through the gathering darkness. Amo'n would have been utterly lost had the old man not had been wreathed by an odd light—a bluish light, it seemed, which caught the sunlight, and glowed in the moonlight. But the oddest thing was, it seemed to glow strongest in the darkness—this light that could never be extinguished. It never dwindled, always persevered.

But now the two of them were small and helpless beneath the shadows of the great oaks, until the old man stood and spoke. "Behold, the Great Forest!"

Amo'n gazed at the great oaks with wonder. Their roots splayed out about the forest floor, and they went far, down into the deeps where none dared venture. And then the voice came again, carried on the wind, but clearer than ever before. Amo'n could feel torment and pain, even death. But he continued to stumble along wearily, beneath the shadow of the oaks, until he and the old man stopped to rest. Though Amo'n appeared to be asleep he was restless and very much awake. He watched the old man study the skies for a long while, reading the clouds with a grim look upon his face until the moon was shrouded by shadow.

The next morning Amo'n and the old man set off again after a cold breakfast of Machu` beans. They walked beneath the cover of trees for many

long hours, until at last they stopped to rest beneath a great oak. Without knowing exactly how he knew, Amo'n was sure the tree had once been of many hues. Now it was dark and bare and plain, alike to all its kin, and it seemed to contain some darkness, a very evil darkness, that had laid the forest bare. Few lights could pierce it. But deep within the trees themselves, in that forest of old, there lay a great light. For many years the darkness had withheld that light, and the darkness itself had sprung from the light.

As he sat beneath the great oak, Amo'n heard the whispering voice once more. It seemed to be near, and it came from all directions—Amo'n could feel darkness encroaching upon him. But then the old man turned, and gave him a long glance, and the strange light that had glimmered all about the old man the previous night had returned. Amo'n was greatly comforted.

The old man wished to escape the forest by dawn of the next day, to make it to the place where the "great wealth" lay. So, Amo'n and the old man soon set off again.

They continued, walking for a long while, until Amo'n's legs grew very weary. He was feeling very cold and weak, and now the sun was falling in the sky. It grew even darker. He now felt as though many eyes were boring down upon his back. He turned but saw nothing save great trees looming up behind him. And then the voice returned, clearer than ever before. His whole body went limp and he felt death and harshness. And then once more he saw the light that encircled the old man, immediately followed by shadow. And Amo'n's mind filled with thoughts of his old home. He snagged his foot upon a stone, stumbled, and lay on the ground for what seemed a long while. Finally, he lifted himself to his feet once more. The old man was a small distant shape, but Amo'n gained new energy as he gazed at the old man. He hurried to catch up.

Amo'n and the old man walked well through the night, and through

a little of the day. At last they came to open fields, and now Amo'n saw light everywhere. He knew the treasure must be growing near.

He inquired of the old man "Where does the treasure lie?"

"Amo'n, what treasure do you seek, one buried beneath this field? There is treasure all around you, in you, is that not a great wealth?"

"You mean there was... nothing?!" cried Amo'n. "I trusted you and you cheated me, tore me from all I have ever known!"

Dark thoughts came to Amo'n, weakening him. And he thought again of his old home. *I have no one I can trust! I am alone! But there must be something... it is over! I have no one to trust! But, no! It cannot be! I have no one I can trust!* And then he collapsed. Everything went dark and he knew no more.

When Amo'n awoke he was lying in the grass. The sky above was golden and the old man was leaning over him. And suddenly Amo'n understood, understood why the old man had brought him on the journey. Suddenly all his fears were gone, and he felt joy and confidence in himself.

"I am sorry!" he cried and began to sob.

"Fear naught," said the old man. "I understand. And now I shall bring you back. I hope you have yet gained something on this journey, for I like to believe I am a man of my word."

And so, they traveled back through the Great Forest, but now everything seemed lighter.

All the darkness left Amo'n and the voice dwindled. And even through the slums the journey felt better, knowing that he was homeward bound. And so, the old man delivered Amo'n to his doorstep, and there he stood.

"Farewell, good Amo'n. Maybe again we will meet."

But no longer was the old man the strange wanderer in his yellow raincoat and blue boots that had walked these roads what seemed an eternity ago. He was now something more, something that had brought light to Amo'n's

life. And then, quite suddenly, the old man was gone.

Amo`n looked at 1857 Dalter Street, and he saw the old rusted door, and the one little window, and the place on the right wall where the paint was flecking off, but now he saw something in his home he had never seen before. And Amo`n stood upon his front doorstep, breathed in deeply, and listened to the rain softly thrumming upon the shingles on the roof.

THE END

Epilogue:

Amo`n and the old man never met again in life, but Amo`n's confidence helped his family rise out of poverty. They bought a nicer house in a nicer place, but now Amo`n trusted himself and others and even began to see the beauty in 1857 Dalter Street.

Character Details

Victoria Cui worked with mentor, Megan White, to revise her story, *Wishes,* with a focus on adding specific character details.

Dear Reader,

    Victoria's story brought to life a character that is struggling with learning differences and feeling like an outcast. Stories like this are so important, bringing forward experiences that people are too willing to ignore. For revision, we focused on how to make this story live up to its potential in terms of character.

    Especially when writing from the perspective of a character with any sort of perspective readers aren't used to, it's important to make sure there are enough **character details** that the reader can really connect to them. This sounds a little counterintuitive; if you want readers to connect to a character, wouldn't you want them to be pretty generalized, so that anyone can fit themselves into the story? But actually, it's those really specific little details about a character that make them feel like a real person, and lets readers connect with them either because they also experience that tiny detail, or because they don't, and that's a connection all on its own!

We started with the main character, Kayla. Obviously, a narrator is the most important in a story like this. Victoria thought about how to bring this character come to life; was her desk messy or neat? How did she hide her books? This story is partially about how her learning differences alienated her, so we wanted to show those details so the reader could see it for themselves, rather than just believing the narrator when she said it.

After that, we talked about secondary characters. Many of them were archetypal, which means that they didn't have the depth of detail and personality that Kayla did. This can seem perfectly fine in a story, but filling out your secondary characters as much as your main ones makes a story more rich and rewarding for a reader. Victoria found, as she started the process of turning a character that was just a "mean girl" into a character with more depth, that enriching the back stories of side characters can actually make the path of the main character more interesting.

A good place to brainstorm character details is with character worksheets. Whether you use actual worksheets with questions about a character or just a blank page to write out parts of a back story in a narrative form, piecing together characters like they're real people makes a huge difference to a story. Most of these details won't actually go into the final draft, as Victoria discovered, but the sense of the character the author gains by coming up with all of that detail shapes their actions and words throughout the story.

Happy writing,

Megan White

Megan White graduated with a major in creative writing from Skidmore, in New York. She grew up writing and hopes to work in publishing someday. She has been a part of the Society of Young Inklings since she was seven years old! Her hobbies include hiking, reading, writing, and getting lost in the depths of Netflix.

Victoria Cui

Victoria Cui is a fourth grader at Phillips Brooks School. She loves golfing, spending time with family, reading, and writing. She wants to be an author someday when she grows up. She loves writing in her spare time and loves adventure.

Megan White: How was the revision process for you? What were your favorite and least favorite parts?

Victoria Cui: My favorite part was seeing it all come together after all the revision I had done. My least favorite was the part where I had to think about a lot of things and consider which ones to include and which ones to discard. I really thought about my theme and what I wanted to deliver through my story, and that kind of guided me through what I wanted to keep and what I thought wouldn't match the story.

Q: How much did you end up changing? Were you surprised by that?

A: I ended up changing a lot of the things, because I felt like some things didn't fit, and I had to include lots of different things to improve the way my story flowed. I expected to just change a little bit, I thought it was good as it was, but then I saw how much it could improve, and I wanted to make it the best story I could make it, so I ended up changing quite a bit!

Q: What advice do you have for writers who don't really like revising?

A: Revision isn't my favorite process either… I think it helps to think about the things that drive your story forward. If they're just details you think fit well or are really cool, don't include it, because you really want something that is going to be delivered through your story and push it forward.

Q: How do you come up with your ideas?

A: I usually look around and get ideas from the world around me, from my friends and from nature, from many different places and aspects of my life. I think if you want to start a story, look around yourself and think about something interesting you might want to write about.

Q: Where is your favorite place to write?

A: My favorite place to write is my front yard. There are a bunch of trees, and I take this little stool and my clipboard and I just write. It's time away from my iPad, and I feel like every time I look at a screen, I see things differently than I do when they're written out. Sometimes it gives me inspiration, because I get to see more things. I can feel trapped sitting in this room just looking outside, being able to see all of it but not feel it.

Wishes

by

Victoria Cui

The sea rushes in and out, and I can feel the cool, bubbly ocean water splashing against my legs. The morning breeze tingles my skin. I just stand there as the sea seems to be calling, *Come in! Come in!*

My chocolate-brown hair flaps in the wind, my toes digging into the wet sand. Desolate and pure, this beach is special. This is the only part of my day I enjoy. Hearing the waves rock and the wind puff calms me and brings the ultimate gift, a sense of acceptance and love. In everything else, I'm the outcast or the failure, in school, at home, the list goes on and on forever.

The seagulls wake and squawk at the sea, seeming to say good morning. I smile and remember the time when my sister and I used to play along the shore and collect the smooth seashells washed in by the tide. The scallop and the sundial, the conch and moon shells, all lying in the sunlight. Now, my sister is busy with things I don't know of and can't play with me anymore.

I stare at the beautiful, open sea as the sun rises in the bright sky, full of red and orange stripes, all seeming to be dancing across space above. The sea, blue and green and hints of silver in it, bobs up and down up and down.

Taking one last glance at the truly sublime ocean stretched in front of me, I walk along the shore back to my house—a plain little brown cottage where my mom was preparing breakfast and my dad was reading his newspaper.

My sister had already left for school. I plopped down in the seat next to my dad and poked my fork in the waffle my mom had prepared for me. I took out the viscid maple syrup and thanked my mom. She smiled, her classical mother one. I smiled back. I finished my waffle, pushed the plate to the edge of the table, and climbed up the stairs, heading into my room. I packed my backpack with my special books and I stuffed them in the very back of my tiny backpack. I knew I was going to get teased at school and I winced at the thought. Another day of taunting and teasing.

I stuffed my folder with the things I needed, my homework, my pencil box, my flashcards and lined paper. I didn't care that my paper was crinkled or that my pencil lead was dull. I just needed to get to class.

I pulled out my fluffy jacket from the closet and said to my mom, "Bye, I'm leaving!"

"Bye, sweetheart." She pulled me into a hug and I hugged her back.

I grabbed my bike and helmet from the shed and started pedaling down the sandy road. The wind had died down but it was cold outside. It wasn't even 5:00 yet. I had to bike since our family didn't have a car. We lived about 17 miles away from the nearest school. When I arrived, I hung my helmet at the bike rack. Sliding off my bike, I heard the bell ring just seconds after I walked into the hallways. I hurried to my locker, plopping my backpack in the cubby and making sure it was zipped tightly. I didn't want anyone to see those books I had brought. When I walked into Room 29, everybody was sitting at their seats and had their green English textbooks open.

"Ah, Miss Johnson, good of you to join us. We are reviewing what we learned yesterday in English." Mr. Marcus's tone was clear he wasn't happy

about me being late.

"Sit down in your seat and open up your textbook to page 102."

I tramped to my seat, like a controlled robot. I fumbled through my messy desk, trying to find my textbook in a jumble of supplies. Finally, I found it in the very back of my desk and I opened it to page 102. The review page was about idioms and cliches. I stared out the window, daydreaming. I knew I wouldn't be able to read it, so I didn't bother.

My mind floated away to Wonderland. I learned this stuff last year at my grandma's. Like my parents, she was accepting and brought me into the family. Grandma always understood. She knew when I was happy and when I wasn't. She is a retired teacher, lives in Boise, and taught me a lot of what I know today. Last year, Grandma taught me by teaching me a little song. It was stuck in my head all summer. I miss Grandma. We can't visit her because we can't afford it. We still have Facetime calls and write letters but it's not the same.

Mr. Marcus was still talking, but I just couldn't focus on his words. I sat there and let my mind take off, up and away, like a plane on the runway. Besides, when I looked at the page my head started to throb and shake. I go to Hellenwood Elementary School in Bentonville, Arkansas. I am in 5th grade. I used to always try to pay attention but it never worked. My mind would wander and follow its own trail, pulling me along with it. I don't try as hard anymore because I bet, even if my life depended on it, I still wouldn't be able to focus.

"Class!" Mr. Marcus's piercing tone popped my daydream bubble and my ears ached from the loudness. I whisked my head to where he was standing.

"All right, sit on the rug, 5B. We are going to greet each other and then head to the study hall."

Everybody scurried to the rug and sat down. My ear drums did not like the volume. They were not pleased.

"All right kids, shake the person's hands next to you and say good morning."

"Hi," I mumbled to Sydney, the girl next to me.

Her blonde curls bounced off her sky blue shirt.

She stuck her tongue at me, not even shaking my hand, and said, "Hey, Kailie."

"It's Kayla. I just reminded you yesterday." I hissed, annoyed.

Every morning she acted like she'd forgotten my name, and then I remind her even though I know she's faking it.

Sydney stuck her tongue out at me and turned away, whispering to her friends on the other side of her. I knew she would do something like that. I pretended to shake it off like any other water drop but it still stuck to my feelings.

Why is she always like this? I thought.

I felt myself boiling up. Hotter and hotter. But then, I calmed down, squeezing my cute emoji squishy I kept in my pocket. After my mood level dropped, I turned around and muttered a hi to Aaron, the boy that sat on the other side of me. He was like a shell with a crack. He was very discreet, keeping to himself most of the time. Like the time in Kindergarten, when we were asked to say something about ourselves. Aaron just said that he had a cat while Sydney droned on about her dog and her chickens and her adorable bunny and her annoying sister. Aaron wasn't always so closed up though, sometimes he would express himself. Other times, he wouldn't. That was him.

"Good morning, Kayla," he simply said.

Aaron turned to listen to what Mr. Marcus was saying.

"All right, let's grab our iPads and line up, " Mr. Marcus said.

I yanked off my charging cord and slid out my iPad. I plopped myself in line and waited for Mr. Marcus to lead us to the study hall. There, I opened my iPad and pulled up my Google Drive.

I heard the meanest girl in the grade, Juliana, whisper to her best friend, Evelyn, "I figured out Kayla's password when she logged in to her Drive. I'm going to hack her account."

She laughed, making sure no one other than her friends heard her. I was horrified. Juliana was so mean. In first grade, we were playing a game and whoever won out of all the students in the class got extra recess. It was the final round, determining who would win.

When it looked like she had lost to me she yelled, "Kayla cheated!" and even though I denied it, saying I could never have cheated, the teacher still sent me home.

Juliana had always gotten her way, whether I objected or I didn't. Another time, on pajama day in third, I brought my favorite stuffy, a black cat named Aurora. A couple of kids voted to see whose stuffy was the cutest out of all the stuffed animals the class owned. When they picked Aurora over Juliana's stuffy, a dog named Tiffany, Juliana grabbed scissors and cut all my cat's hair. I cried and she called me a crybaby.

Forgetting to control my temper, I yelled at her, saying, "Juliana, you are *NOT* going to hack my account! I don't want you to, so please don't."

I looked into her brown eyes. But then, she just threw back her head and laughed again. All the students in the room had closed their iPads and stared at us, the eyes darting from Juliana to me again and again going in a loop back and forth.

After a long pause, Juliana pulled out her phone and said, "Who says I can't?"

I ran over and ripped the phone from Juliana's grasp. I threw it on the ground, and the glass shattered into hundreds of tiny pieces. I stared at the broken phone—I didn't mean to break anything. I realized that I was being like Juliana, and felt ashamed of myself. By this time, Mr. Marcus had returned from the teacher's lounge.

He said, "Kayla, you are coming with me to the office."

"But…," I protested.

"No buts."

I followed him to Ms. Anderson's office, chin drooping.

Apparently, the principal wasn't there. Mr. Marcus told me to get my backpack and go home. I tried to explain what had happened but he wouldn't listen. I asked him why he was sending me home.

"You were disrupting others," was the only answer I got.

"Hey! Did you hear what Juliana said? I don't know why everything is so unfair!" I yelled.

I got home just as my mom came outside to water the plants in the garden bed near our kitchen window.

She saw me and asked, clearly surprised, "Why home this early, little bug?"

"I don't exactly want to talk about it."

Mom nodded. She looked like she wanted to say something but what fell out of her lips was only an "okay."

When I put my backpack down, I saw Brownie, my Labradoodle dog, chomping on his bone I had given him in the morning. I went up to my room and I flopped down on my bed.

Why does school have to be so hard? I thought. But I knew I only had trouble in school because of my learning differences. I was born with Dyslexia and ADHD. I wished I could be more normal, like other kids. I often lose my temper because I feel like everything is all tilted, not always fair. I'd tell my classmates why I had such a hard time. I wish I could be smarter. It would be so much easier. But those are just wishes.

I walked to the place I had always loved, the beach near my house. Nobody ever comes to the beach and it's literally my second home. I feel like it belongs to me. My toes dug into the sandy shore as the waves crashed against

the rocks among the sea.

As I stared out into the waters I thought, *Am I always going to lose my temper this way? I will try to be a person that can help others, and I will certainly try to be the best I can be.*

Heart of a Poem

Lila Tierney worked with mentor, Desiree Middleton, to focus on the heart of her poem in her revision of this piece, *A Note in Time*.

Dear Reader,

Lila focused on editing her poem, *A Note in Time*, from the perspective of drawing out the **heart of the poem**.

What does the heart of the poem mean? It means the thread that runs through your poem that pulls the reader along on an emotional journey. Because Lila also plays piano, we decided to approach her editing from a musical standpoint.

Our hearts beat changed based on our mood. We looked at changing some of the words in her lines based on music signatures like mf and mp, and crescendo and decrescendo. Lila was able to give her poem rises and falls like a heartbeat based on her love of music.

As you edit your next poem, think about seeing your words as a piece of music. Every music piece has soft and loud parts, rises and falls ... just like a heartbeat.

Happy writing,
Desiree Middleton

Desiree Middleton is an award-winning screenwriter who loves creating imaginative worlds and characters to fill them. She is addicted to Twinkies and resides in Los Angeles.

Lila Tierney

Lila is in sixth grade at Metropolitan Learning Center in Portland, Oregon. She loves trees, plants, animals and enjoys simply being in nature. Lila likes to draw and has a passion for ballet and tap dancing. She also plays violin, accordion and piano, which is what inspired her to write this poem. Lila would like to become a paleozoologist and writer/illustrator. She is intrigued by history, especially natural history, and is thrilled by the unexplained. Right now, she favors the classical and elegant in almost any genre; clothing, taste, arts, and style. Her favorite place to be is on a stage acting, singing… doing almost anything. She does not have pets, but instead fosters kittens from the local Humane Society.

Desiree Middleton: Tell us about your revision process.
Lila Tierney: It felt shorter than expected, but effective. Mentors aren't trying to make the poem different, but help to make it better.

Q: What advice would you give other Inklings who don't enjoy the revision process?
A: Don't think you can't make it better because now I see that revision gives you a lot of opportunities. Imagine you're not making your writing different, but you're switching around the words. The mentors are there to help but you're the one who decides to change your poem or not.

Q: When did you begin writing?

A: I think in pictures. I've been thinking and talking in pictures ever since I was four. Mom told me it was poetry. I've wanted to be a writer since I was eight or nine.

Q: What poems or stories do you think you'll work on next?

I'm already writing a promising story about an imaginative adult with flashbacks. The story is realistic fiction with internal monologue. It might end up as a novella.

A Note in Time

by

Lila Tierney

I am the queen's piano from regal times of olde,
My ivory is the best in the land.
I'm strung magnificently, I'm told,
And carved from beech by hand.

My pedals are of beaten brass,
Though polished 'til they're gold.
My keys once wooed the upper class,
But now they're still and cold.

I am a worthy instrument—
Worthy of attention.
I yearn for praise, a compliment,
Yet, I receive no mention.

Will I ever again be swept up in song, trilling a lively allegretto along?

Then one day while waiting there,
A discerning eye observes and peeps.
And over to my dusty lair,
A little figure creeps.

She looks at me. I look at her,
And then she starts to speak.
But it's been so long, I do concur...
What if my tone is weak?

She sensed the woe I tried to hide,
Yet leaves me reassured.
Onto my wooden bench she slides.
At last, my call is heard!

Oh it's been so long since my cover's been lifted,
and longer still since my music's been sifted.

Her agile, slender fingers
Dance upon my keys.
Through octaves, slurs, and lingers
With elegance and ease.

The melodic harmony does allure.
It frees me from my prideful code.
No need for stage, nor rich grandeur,
Just the joy of a child's ode.

My ivory may be slightly worn.
Hushed is my soprano.
But my happiness now is born,
For I'm a child's piano.

Active Verbs

Jubilee Close worked with mentor, Ailynn Knox-Collins, on a revision of *Thalassophilia*, that focused on adding even more movement and energy to Jubilee's compelling story.

Dear Reader

Jubilee's story, *Thalassophilia*, moves us through a long period of the character's life. Many things happen to her over the years. So for revision, we decided to revise for **active verbs**.

Verbs help to move the story, both literally and figuratively. Strong verbs help readers to see what the writer sees in her head as she wrote the story. The way the characters move through the plot, the reactions from others and the setting, are all made vivid with strong verbs.

First, we looked at the sentences in the story that needed to paint a vivid picture in the reader's mind.

For example,
"My friends stare back, showing their teeth in an attempt to seem happy and affectionate."

Instead of using *showing*, Jubilee replaced her verb with bare.

"My friends stare back, teeth bared. They appear happy and affectionate…"

Second, we decided to remove all the unnecessary adverbs. Replacing them with strong verbs gives readers a clearer picture.

For example:

"Light pitifully attempts to break through from behind…"

Was revised to become:

"Light breaks through from behind…"

Third, Jubilee looked at filter phrases and removed many of them. Filters are phrases like "began to," "it seemed as if," "almost," "she saw," "she heard," etc. Taking out filters allows the verbs to play their role. The sentences sound more immediate and the reader is right there with the character.

For example, in the sentence above, the writer removed "attempts to." Now, as the light breaks through, it feels more immediate, and it creates a stronger picture.

Here are some more examples:

- "Excuses began spilling out of my mouth" feels more immediate if we say: "Excuses spilled out of my mouth."
- "My friends don't understand. I try to tell them how the ocean wouldn't take him…" was revised to: "My friends don't understand. I tell them how the ocean wouldn't take him…"

In both cases, the removal of the filter made the action feel more immediate. The reader stays that much closer to what's going on in the story.

Finally, in revision, we also talked about the use of the simple present tense. When writing in the present tense, often the simple version of the tense is the most powerful. The occasional use of the progressive is acceptable, but I challenge you, as a writer to try the sentence in the simple tense. See if that sounds stronger. Very often it will.

Keep writing,

Ailynn Knox-Collins

Ailynn Knox-Collins has been a Montessori teacher for many years and loves sharing her love of books and writing with her students. She has an MFA in Writing for Children and Young Adults from Hamline University. She is the author of several books for young and middle grade readers—mainly science fiction and nonfiction stories. When she's not writing, she is working with her five dogs on agility, obedience, and rally competitions. She is excited to mentor with Young Inklings and share her love for writing with young authors everywhere.

Jubilee Close

Jubilee Close is a ninth grader at Live Oak Academy in California. She writes as much as she possibly can and always listens to music while doing so. She's a huge K-Pop fan. Her family and friends jokingly describe her interests as "death and destruction" since she tends to like the darker aspects of plots. Her favorite characters are almost always sub-villains. The item at the very top of her bucket list is to visit Croatia.

Ailynn Knox-Collins: What are your favorite books?

Jubilee Close: I like the *Renegades* series by Marissa Meyer, the *Ms. Peregrine* series by Ransom Riggs, and *Fahrenheit 451*.

Q: What draws you to these types of books?

A: It's different for each. I like their writing styles and the stories. If it's interesting with unique characters, I enjoy them. For example, Bradbury's style is unlike anything I've seen before—how he uses verbs in a way that people don't usually use them.

Q: What do you like to write?

A: I like stories that have an ensemble of characters. I like it when they start out not knowing each other, and they come together in the story to complete the plot.

Q: When did you start writing?

A: I've been writing for as long as I can remember. There was one time when I was very young, in Kindergarten I think, where I had a grand idea for a story. I couldn't write so I dictated it to my dad who wrote it for me. It's a one-page story.

Q: What made you write this particular story?

A: I take Latin, and in the 8th grade we were translating a passage. The first sentence was *"I was sailing on trusted winds, but I was anxious."* I wanted to write something based on that sentence.

Originally, it was a flash fiction piece. My goal was to challenge myself to use more metaphors and to write deeper description. It ended up being around 300 words. After I wrote it, I entered it into a Nanowrimo contest. I didn't win or anything. I put it away. Then when I worked with Sonja through Society of Young Inklings for this contest, I expanded the story. But the story I ended up entering was actually the backstory of the main character in the flash fiction.

Q: What changed after you revised?

A: I worked on refining the verbs and taking away the filters, making the emotional side of the story more powerful.

Q: Do you enjoy revision?

A: I enjoy the first revision. I'm a person who revises while I write. I like that. But revising after it's finished, it's weird because it feels as if it's already set. As I revise, I like to read through the story as a reader. I get excited about it and I want to make it better.

Q: What are you working on next?

A: I started working on a novel in 2018. I'm still working on it. It's about six people who get stuck on an apartment floor, and they're being terrorized by a killer. I also write a lot of stories at the same time.

Q: Who do you share your stories with?

A: It depends on the story; some are really secret. I have my best friend, with whom I share all my writings. Sometimes, when I'm still working on something, I share it with my friend and my sister. They give good feedback. I'm really secretive about some of my stories.

Thalassophilia

by

Jubilee Close

I clap my hands, excited beyond my days as the sailboat lifts off of the shore and begins bobbing over the waves into the vast sea. Daddy always said how he would take me sailing when I was old enough, and now I finally am! Nine years old, and ready to face the ocean!

"This is so cool!" I look up at Daddy as he works the ropes and sails.

"Isn't it?" he chuckles.

Giggling at my surroundings, I crane over the edge of the boat and run my hand down the smooth side.

"Careful, now, Caroline!" Daddy warns.

"I know! I just want to touch the water!"

"Wait until we're farther out, when the currents aren't as strong. Then you can, I promise!"

Understanding, I retreat from the edge and pick my way over to the front of the boat. The wind tickles through my hair teasingly, blowing blonde strands in front of my face. I've dreamt of this day for oh so long! When I was very little, I watched my daddy sail out into the ocean, and I knew I wanted to be out there with him.

This is where I'm meant to be. I just know it.

The shore is small in the distance. Daddy says it is safe to touch the water now. I hop up and lean over, making sure to keep a good grip on the boat with one hand. The tips of my fingers graze the water. It's so cold! It sends shivers up my arm, but I like it. I let my entire hand sink into the water and laugh.

Daddy appears next to me. "Having fun?"

"Yes!"

"What do you see?"

I stick out my bottom lip and squint at the blackening swells. "It's too dark."

"Then, what do you feel?"

"It's very cold!" I exclaim.

"How about this: What do you hear?"

I snort at his ridiculous statement. "It's water! It doesn't really make noise…" I trail off as a snatch of a whisper scatters past my ear. I bolt upright, searching for the source. "What was that?"

"Did you hear something?"

"I– I–" There it is again. A light breath of forbidden knowledge. An invitation to delve into the unknown. I rush to the other end of the boat and slam against the side to peer over, almost losing my balance.

The swirls of the sea form shapes that I cannot comprehend. Voices dangle just beneath the surface which I desperately want to encounter. I yearn to know them. I yearn for them to know *me*. But they dance just out of reach.

"Caroline?!" My dad sounds worried.

I turn to him. "Yes?"

"You're pale as snow!"

"I am?"

He sinks to his knees in front of me and grasps my shoulders, dark brows furrowed in concern. "What happened?"

I stare back at him, mouth parted. "The sea voices called to me, and I wanted to answer."

"The sea voices?"

"Yes! But I can't get to them."

He looks off to the horizon, not responding.

"I want to answer them, Daddy!"

"You do?"

"I've never wanted anything so much in my entire life!"

He doesn't quite understand, but I am telling the truth.

"Hey, Dad?"

He turns his head to me before going back to working the ropes. "Yes?"

"How dangerous is sailing, really?"

I've been thinking about this for a while. It's been about four years since we've started sailing together. We share a love for the ocean, and our trips have always been just that. Love.

Lately, though, I've started seeing things differently. I gaze at the water and no longer just see the playful waves. I peer past the frisky currents and catch sight of the depths. Those depths are dark. It puts me on edge. I doubt the depths would ever actually manifest evil, but the possibility seems a bit too within reach.

"Sailing can be very dangerous," he answers.

I look back at the darkness. "Then why do you love it?"

"Why do *you* love it?" he retorts with his wide grin.

I shrug. "It's pleasant. And I enjoy it. I feel at home."

"Exactly. Just because something is dangerous doesn't mean it's bad."

Nodding, I balance on the rim of the boat and trail my fingertips along the surface of the water.

"The safety of the ocean lies in the danger of the waters."

"That doesn't really make any sense," I snicker.

He laughs too. "But it sure sounds cool, doesn't it?"

Once more, I peer into the depths and now I see clearly. I see that I was wrong. The depths are not dangerous. They are misunderstood.

The school bus drops me off at the corner and I lug my stuff along the sidewalk to my house. I hike my knee up once again to keep the sleeping bag from falling out of my grip. My arms are so full I kick the door instead of knocking.

My mom opens it almost immediately. I look up at her and grin. But my smile falters. Her eyes are puffy and red. Her hair is uncombed.

"What's wrong?" I ask alarmedly.

"Come in," she says softly.

I shuffle into the house and dump my things next to the shoe rack. I'll take care of that later.

My mom guides me to sit on the living room couch. She sits next to me, taking my hand, her grip shaky. "Honey, you know that sailing trip with Dad you had to cancel because of the camp?"

Her tone troubles me. "Yes?"

"He—he went sailing with Uncle Jack instead, and…" She takes a deep breath and squeezes my hand, "He didn't come back."

The words linger in the air for a few prolonged moments before striking my soul.

Excuses spill out of my mouth. "No! He just wanted to stay at sea longer. Or he got lost! I bet he's on his way back now! Or... or..."

"Uncle Jack came back yesterday." She holds my gaze lovingly, trying to soften the blow with her loving touch.

"But how did it happen? How— how— I don't-"

"Uncle Jack woke up one day and he was gone."

"But he's *Dad*, he can't have drow— he can't... he..." I collapse into sobs, falling into my mother's arms. She envelops me and presses her lips to the top of my head. I give in to the comfort, hoping it will warm me.

She holds me tight, but I feel cold.

I grab a fistful of blanket as thoughts swarm my mind once more.

How could this have happened? It doesn't make sense.

The ocean is *with* him, it is on his side. The waters were always good to him. It wouldn't dare take him, not ever.

I sit up, frustration suffocating me. I fling open my window and look out onto the glistening sea.

The moonlight sparkles against the waves.

The ocean is beautiful. Such beauty couldn't possibly claim a life on purpose.

The cold air pierces my nose and lungs. It blows at my face and brushes the tears out of my eyes. I glare at the ocean, which I used to love and long for. I still long for it. But I no longer love it.

I hate it now.

It's a thief and a murderer and doesn't care about anything except itself.

I slam the window shut, grinding my teeth. I collapse on the ground and curl my knees to my chest. I want to squeeze out the pain in my soul.

I want to forget about the ocean. I want to reject it completely.

Something deep within me refuses to let go.

For the hundredth time, I smooth down the front of my black skirt. I need to do something with my hands.

I try to sit still on the wooden church pew, the situation is too overwhelming. The slideshow displays photo after photo of *him*. He smiles, he laughs. I want to reach out and grasp him. He's right there, so real.

My mom scooches closer to me and squeezes my hand. It seems to be a habit of hers nowadays. She gazes at me. I meet her eyes and she smiles sadly.

She squeezes tighter, whispering, "I love you."

But the words mean nothing to me.

People go on stage and talk of him, speaking flowery words that bring tears to eyes. They say wonderful things.

We were supposed to sail through life together. Why did I ever think that a camp was more important than a sailing trip? I should have been there with him. We would be together where we belong.

They say his body sank to the ocean floor, damp and dead. If only I could have grabbed him as he fell. If only we had gone down together.

If only we could have savored the ocean together *forever.*

My classmates whisper about me. I hear them. They think I don't, but I do. They think that I'm off the edge now, the crazy daughter of a crazy sailor. My friends don't understand. I try to tell them how the ocean wouldn't take him, that the ocean was acting out of character. They brush it off and tell me that they're always there for me. But how can they truly comfort me if they ignore what I insist upon?

Do they *actually care?*

Two picture frames sit on my nightstand. One a silver metal, displaying a snapshot of me and my friends with ice cream. The other a blue painted wood, portraying me and my dad on a sunny day nine years ago, covered in sand and beaming.

I stare at them.

My friends stare back, teeth bared. They tried to seem happy and affectionate.

Now I see right through their masks.

My dad stares back, eyes still twinkling at me. That twinkle never once left his gaze and never will.

I clutch the metal frame and narrow my eyes. My grip intensifies. My knuckles grow white. I hurl the frame against the wall. The glass shatters and the frame falls to the floor. I tiptoe towards the broken object. The photo is dislodged. I snatch it up. My fingers shake and I rip it in half. Then I rip it again. And again. I rip through their pretty faces. I open the window and cast the fragments out, where the wind catches them and they drift away from me.

I let them go.

I haven't opened the curtains for weeks. The black drapes hang mournfully over the window, shielding me in my solitude. Light attempts to break through, but I won't let it touch me. The light is painful. I won't let it touch me.

My legs are numb from sitting on the floor for hours. My neck aches from not lifting my head. I hug my knees closer to my chest and press them onto my eyelids.

Tears threaten to squeeze through the threads that sew my eyes shut. I'm absent from myself. My soul has left me. It's sunk to the ocean floor along with… along with…

The threads snap. Salty droplets waterfall down my cheeks and leave throbbing trails.

The door of my room creaks slightly. I startle and look up to see my mother opening the door. She gazes at me with a furrowed brow.

"Honey? Are you–"

"I'm fine!" I wipe my eyes and will myself not to cry.

She starts to walk forward. I stand, not making eye contact. My joints crack from the sudden movement and I wince. She gently places her arm over my shoulders.

"You don't need to act brave. You can talk to me."

I shake my head. "No, I'm good. I just, I don't know… I don't…"

Despite my efforts not to, I burst into tears. She squeezes my shoulders tighter, wrapping me in a protective hug. It feels wrong.

I make a choice. I reject her embrace. My mother's arms no longer ease the pain. They now tighten the chains. The chains chafe the crevices

of my heart. I wince and start coughing. The arms slip off of me. I want my mother to go and she does. The door slinks shut. My eyes turn away. I sink back to the floor and dig my heels into the carpet.

Darkness chokes the edges of my sight.

I stand on the shoreline, looking out into the sea. Cold water laps at my toes and I shiver. I've stood on this spot almost every day for the past three years. Why do I keep coming back? The ocean should be an enemy, right?

As I look out at the waves, a sentence whistles through my mind, a detached memory.

The safety of the ocean lies in the danger of the waters.

He loved the ocean. He probably still loves it. I can't imagine him not loving it. It's not who he is. Years ago, I couldn't imagine myself not loving it. He couldn't imagine it either. How would he react if he saw me now? His daughter, scared, grieving, conflicted. Holding a grudge against our greatest love. He would be disappointed.

My eyes rest on the familiar sailboat floating in the shallows and moored to the dock. The mast sticks up regally like a beacon, calling to me. It knows I want to become one with it again. I can barely stand it.

I scrape up a handful of wet sand and throw it as hard as I can. It breaks apart and disappears into the water. That's exactly how I feel. The shattered pieces of my heart are skipping into the ocean and I desperately want to chase after them.

I eye the sailboat once more.

What would he want for me? He would want me to be happy. He would want me to feel safe.

Where do I feel safe? Where did *he* feel safe?

I smile, knowing what I have to do.

Before I know it, my arms are full of supplies and necessities and I am loading them into the boat and raising the sails. I pause while unmooring the boat. Am I really doing this? After so long avoiding the ocean?

Yes. It's what he would want. It's what *I* want. I can't deny my love any longer.

I let the rope fall, and the sailboat drifts away, disconnecting me from the land and bringing me home.

Setting Details

Aidan Felt worked with mentor, Megan White, on a revision focused on adding setting details in Aidan's story, *Time Trip*.

Dear Reader,

Aidan's story takes place in Ancient Greece, and takes the narrator through the experience of time travel. When you are writing a story like this, it is important to ground your reader in a strong sense of place. Your reader wants to see and feel the difference between our own time and an ancient one.

This story already had a strong sense of character and growth, so being able to immerse the reader in the historical setting brought the story up to a whole new level. Most readers are already familiar with settings like museums and Ancient Athens, so why is it important to include so much detail? Because the details you choose can make a story your own. Show your readers how *you* see this world you have created, and how the setting influences your characters.

Setting details also help make the plot more tense and interesting. If the reader is grounded in the sensory details of the story, if they can feel the earth and the air, then they'll feel much more attached to the action and the characters. Think of the five senses; if you can find specific details that connect to all of them, you'll feel like you're in the world with the characters, rather than just reading about them!

As you add all this detail, consider your plan for how to include it all. Aidan was already successfully describing locations, particularly Xerxes's house, but sometimes stopping to describe a setting for a paragraph when a character walks into a new place feels stilted for the reader. There are times when this is a good strategy, but it can be good to mix things up. The new way we tried adding detail was through action. We looked at scenes like the fight with Heracles, and thought about what Joey would have noticed in the moment.

Using this strategy, you can build character and setting at the same time; different characters will notice different things! You can build tension and setting at the same time too, revealing things at key moments or increasing the amount of sensory detail when you want the reader to get really immersed in a moment.

For your own stories, think about how the setting impacts the story. Is the setting a place the reader would be familiar with? In that case, be sure to include enough detail that we can see your own spin on it. Is it a fantasy world you created? Make sure you have enough detail for the reader to see it the way you do. Mix up the ways you reveal these details, and always come back to these questions:

- What is important about the setting to my character in this moment?
- How can I make the reader feel they're in the world of my story?

Happy writing!

Megan White

Megan White graduated with a major in creative writing from Skidmore, in New York. She grew up writing and hopes to work in publishing someday. She has been a part of the Society of Young Inklings since she was seven years old! Her hobbies include hiking, reading, writing, and getting lost in the depths of Netflix.

Aidan Felt

Aidan Felt is in fourth grade at Woodinville Montessori School. He plays soccer and basketball and loves to read and play with his puppy. History and science are his favorite subjects. He doesn't know what he wants to be when he grows up, yet, but he hopes it involves leopards. He likes to travel and hopes to see as much of the world as he can.

Megan White: How was the revision process for you? What were your favorite and least favorite parts?

Aidan Felt: It was actually pretty fun! It was way more fun than actually doing the story, because you got to go back over and rewrite what you've already done, which was pretty cool. That was probably my favorite part. I don't even think I have a least favorite part!

Q: How much did you end up changing? Were you surprised by that?

A: Probably about 5 to 10 things. First of all, I didn't even think I was going to win and revise at all, but I thought I would have a lot more revisions to do than that!

Q: What advice do you have for writers who don't really like revising?

A: That's a really hard question… It's really just about finding a place to start. What I did was just think a lot about where my character was, and add in details based on that.

Q: What's your favorite way to write?

A: Honestly, I prefer to write things out longhand, but this was like a fifteen-page book, and would have taken a lot out of me to write it all out!

Q: How did you come up with the idea for this story?

A: I just really like Greek Mythology, so I just thought it would be fun to do a story about it!

Time Trip

by

Aidan Felt

"Hey Forreester. Walk much?"

Joey Forrester looked up from the slick marble steps he had just wiped out on to see Anthony Giles standing over him, smirking. Anthony was big, mean, had an endless supply of snide comments, and was somehow always around when Joey's awkwardness kicked in. Being eleven wasn't easy. He mentally kicked himself for tripping.

Why can't I be a klutz in private? Joey wondered. *How hard is it to walk and tell time?*

In an instant, the entire class on the museum field trip had turned to look at him and the laughter spread. Joey's shoulders slumped and his face turned red and felt hot. Even the kids he thought were friends seemed to be laughing at him. *Why do they do that? They're just as intimidated by him as I am.*

"Looks like my work here is done," Anthony sneered as he turned and headed up the polished stairs to the Ancient Greece and Rome exhibit.

As the rest of the class shuffled up the stairs, Joey picked himself up, muttered some angry, self-critical comments, and straightened his rumpled clothes. He hung back a few steps from the other kids, but followed them up to

the gallery. Joey could hear his footsteps echoing around the empty first floor, amplifying the noise from his sneakers on the stone steps.

Joey trudged up three flights of stairs, passing several displays along the way. When he finally got to the exhibit, he saw a banner above a revolving door that read: EXHIBIT GRAND OPENING: GREECE AND ROME. The revolving door that led to the exhibit seemed a little odd, since it was the only one in the museum, but Joey didn't give it too much thought.

He pushed on the door and stepped inside. Suddenly, a bright white light enveloped him, and he felt like he was spinning, not the door. He was dizzy, didn't know what was going on, and felt a little sick to his stomach. Just when he thought he might actually get sick, the spinning stopped.

Dazed, Joey pushed slightly on the door. A hot breeze smacked him in the face. The sun was bright in his eyes and, as he squinted to block it out, he heard a lyre playing in the distance. As his eyes adjusted to the light, he spun around and saw that the door was no longer there. In its place was a tall rock spire.

"What the…? This isn't the museum," Joey muttered.

"NO!" boomed a deep voice behind him, "You are in Athens!"

Joey turned to see a tall, muscular man with the rich color of a bronze sculpture looking at him curiously.

"What is your name?" the man asked.

"Uh, I was about to ask you the same thing," said Joey.

"I am Xerxes, son of Xelam," the man said, as if that were supposed to mean something to Joey.

"Um, I'm Joey Forrester, uh…son of…my parents," said Joey. "How did I get here? And how do I get home? What's going on?"

"This is a trial," Xerxes explained. "Kekrops, King of Athens, requires that all visitors who wish to leave complete three tasks to prove their worth. If

you choose not to test your worth, you must remain in Athens." Joey looked up at Xerxes, who suddenly seemed huge. Or maybe Joey just felt small. "Do you wish to test your worth?"

Seriously?! I just wanted to see the exhibit—I didn't want to be part of it! How am I gonna complete three tasks? I haven't even finished my short story for school! And what kind of tasks? And—

"You must make a choice," Xerxes interrupted Joey's panicked thoughts. "Will you test your worth?"

"I, uh, I—I want to go home," Joey said softly, looking down at his feet.

"Then you must accept the challenge."

Joey tried to think of a way to get out of this. Nothing came to mind.

"I, uh, well, I guess, then, uh, yes. I guess I'll test my worth," Joey said. *What worth?*

"A bold decision," Xerxes said, a slight smile on his face. "Your first task will start after the next sunset. Until then, I suggest you rest. You will need all of your strength and cunning to meet the challenges to come."

Joey gulped.

"You are welcome to rest at my home, if you wish."

Xerxes's house was very simple, so Joey was surprised when Xerxes asked him to take off his shoes at the door. The floors were made of grayish white clay that felt smooth and cool under Joey's bare feet. The walls had shelves of ruddy pottery with black decorations that displayed amazing feats of Greek heroes. Joey recognized a *pithos* among the pieces of pottery.

He had learned a little bit about the history of Greece in school. He wondered if that might come in handy later. Xerxes showed him to a small, cozy room with a fire burning in a hearth near the corner. Near the hearth was a mat made of woven reeds and fleece. Joey thanked Xerxes and settled onto the mat. His mind was racing with worry.

How can I possibly do this? I'm just a kid. Strength and cunning? I didn't even ask what happens if I don't complete the challenges. What if all that Greek Mythology stuff is real? What if I have to face Medusa? I can't win against Medusa! I'm dead. Here lies Joey Forrester—he tripped on the stairs and teleported 2,500 years into the past and was turned to stone by a gorgon! One terrible thought after another flew through his head until he couldn't stay awake any longer. He fell asleep, worrying about what the next day would bring.

"Joey Forrester!"

Joey and Xerxes stood in front of Kekrops, King of Athens.

"Xerxes tells me you would like to test your worth by completing the trial of strength, wisdom, and perseverance. Is that correct?"

Joey looked at Xerxes nervously. He didn't really want to do that at all. He didn't have any interest in the trial or the challenges or any of whatever this was that was going on. But he did want to go home.

"Y—yes." Joey barely got the word out. His legs felt weak and the blazing sun made him woozy.

"The rules are simple," boomed Kekrops. "You will have one hour to complete each task. If you fail to complete any of the three tasks, you must remain in Athens. Forever."

Joey didn't like that sound of that.

"Your first task is a demonstration of strength. You must best—"

"My King," interrupted Xerxes, "this challenge is too great. He is only a child! No fully-grown man has ever—"

"Enough!" snapped Kekrops. "He accepted the challenge. Now he must prove himself worthy! Tomorrow, after the sun has cleared Mt. Lykavittos, you must best the strongest of our heroes—Heracles!"

Joey's jaw dropped. Xerxes lowered his head.

That's it, Joey thought, *I'm dead.*

The next morning, Xerxes walked Joey to the magnificent stadium in the center of the city. It was huge, with sandy floors and the faint scent of jasmine. As Joey looked around, he could see row upon row of seating. It was all overwhelming.

"You will need luck today," Xerxes said. Joey rolled his eyes.

"Gee, thanks. How 'bout a miracle? Got any of those?" As they approached the stadium, Joey could hear the crowd. Their shouts grew louder the closer he got. Joey began to feel nauseated. *I can't do this. There's no way I can do this.*

"Strength is not only physical, my friend," said Xerxes. "Keep your wits about you."

Inside the stadium, Kekrops stood on a raised platform. "People of Athens!" he said.

"We have a Visitor!" The crowd went wild and began chanting, "VIS-I-TOR! VIS-I-TOR! VIS-I-TOR!"

"Let the trial begin! The first task is a feat of strength against the heroic Heracles!"

"HER-A-CLES! HER-A-CLES! HER-A-CLES!"

"Bring out our Hero!" Joey's eyes darted around nervously.

An unusually muscular man wearing the hide of a lion stepped out from behind the dais. Joey's eyes widened and his heart nearly stopped. As Heracles strode out, Joey had a sudden flashback to last Halloween, when his family had dressed up as Greek heroes. Except the fake muscles of his costume were nothing compared to this man's. Heracles was enormous—by far the tallest, biggest, most massively oversized human Joey had ever seen—and buff, too. His arms and legs were like a landscape of rolling hills. By the time Joey stopped obsessing over the size of those muscles, Heracles was right next to him, looking down at him. Way down at him. Joey had to crane his neck to see Heracles' face, which was scarred and suntanned.

"Best of luck," Heracles said confidently.

Yep. I'm gonna die. Joey was terrified of what was about to happen. Heracles waved to the crowd as he crossed to the other side of the arena to take his place. The crowd erupted in cheers. After several minutes, Kekrops raised his arm and the crowd quieted down.

"The first task starts… NOW!" Kekrops declared.

Joey panicked when he saw Heracles charging towards him. Joey ran away, trying to vary his path, but Heracles changed direction just as quickly, despite the sand, and barreled towards him. Joey dodged and Heracles came back again. Every time Joey managed to scamper away, Heracles pursued him. Never once did Joey have the upper hand.

The match went on in this way for the better part of an hour. Joey retreated, Heracles pursued. Exhausted and afraid, Joey could feel his time running out. His shoulders slumped and he began to accept that this task was an impossible one. His only hope was not to let Heracles catch up to him. He knew he couldn't beat Heracles. He had to outrun him.

Sensing Joey's weakness, Heracles cornered Joey against the blazing, ten-foot stone wall surrounding the arena and moved to take him down. Joey raised his hands in the air to surrender, hoping the huge man would take pity on him and not crush him. He braced himself for what would come next. As he stretched his arms up, the sun's light suddenly struck the face of the watch on his wrist, bounced off and temporarily blinded Heracles, who closed his eyes to block out the light.

Joey didn't think. He seized his moment, calling on every bit of strength and courage he had left. He rushed at Heracles and threw himself against the giant body. It was like slamming into a brick wall. Surprisingly, Heracles staggered back, off balance, unable to keep himself upright, and fell to the ground with a heavy thud.

Stunned gasps escaped from the crowd.

What just happened? Am I alive?

"Joey Forrester has won the first task…?!" Kekrops was as shocked as the crowd.

Joey shook his head in disbelief and collapsed in a heap on the ground. He looked down at his watch. *Whoa.*

"You have fared well, young visitor! Luck was your friend this day. Rest tonight, for tomorrow your wisdom will be tested by the Sphinx of Thebes!"

The crowd rose to its feet and cheered. Xerxes helped Joey up. Drained of energy, Joey limped out of the arena only to collapse again outside.

"An excellent outcome," said Xerxes.

"How did I do that?" Joey asked.

"Luck. Strength. Wits." Xerxes winked slyly. "And maybe a small miracle." For the first time in two days, Joey could feel himself start to relax.

Joey followed Xerxes back to his house. He took his shoes off at the front door. They shared a meal of grapes, olives, flat bread, and some kind of delicious fish. Exhausted, Joey went directly to bed after dinner.

Joey woke up and stretched on his mat on the floor. He sat up and scratched his head, wondering how tricky the Sphinx's riddle would be. He remembered reading about the Sphinx of Thebes. *I'm pretty sure she eats you if you get the answer to her riddle wrong,* he thought. *They can't do that, can they? Eat a kid? From the future?* The small amount of relief he felt after beating Heracles disappeared.

Xerxes appeared in the doorway.

"You will need to focus today," he offered. "Do not get distracted. Today is not the day to second-guess yourself."

"TODAY is not the day?" asked Joey, raising his voice. "What about every other day?

All I do is second-guess myself!" He fell back on his mat and was quiet for a minute. "How hard is this riddle, Xerxes?" he asked. "Has anyone ever solved it? How many guesses do I get?"

Xerxes glanced away.

"One man solved the riddle."

"Just one?"

"One. You get one guess."

"THAT'S IT??? One lousy guess? One lousy guy?" *This is so messed up. How did I get myself into this?*

"We must go." Xerxes left the room.

Joey slowly got up to follow Xerxes. He tried to stand upright, but his shoulders felt like they were weighed down.

The stadium was packed. When he entered, some of the people in the crowd started cheering. Confused, he looked around to see what they were cheering at. It took him a minute to realize they were cheering for him. Not all the people, but some of them. They were cheering. For him! He thought he felt a tiny bit of confidence building inside him.

Across the arena, Joey saw what looked like a lion with a woman's head and wings. The Sphinx!

"You may approach," said the Sphinx in a rich, melodious voice.

Joey crossed the arena floor and stopped pretty far away from her. *If I'm far enough away, maybe I can run before she eats me,* he thought.

"Closer, child," said the Sphinx.

Joey moved a little closer, shuffling his feet in the sand. He looked up at her. *I wonder what kind of teeth she's got in there. Are they lion teeth or human teeth?*

"Closer."

Oh, this isn't good.

"And now, a riddle: "What can be measured but not seen, felt but not

touched, and can tear down mountains but has no arms?"

Joey furrowed his brow and immediately panicked. His face flushed and he began to sweat. His brain raced a million miles an hour.

Measured but not seen? Rulers, yardsticks, tape measures. No those are things that measure. What can't be seen? Air, invisible ink. No, that's not it. What can you feel but not see? Air. Could it be air? No, you can't really measure air, can you? Air can't tear down a mountain. Can it? Look at those wings. Even if I run, she'll catch me. I have no idea what to say.

Joey stood there for so long, thinking and worrying and thinking some more, that his knees started to buckle. He sat down and stared at the sand. He watched for several minutes as the sun moved across the arena. His shadow slowly changed. He suddenly became aware that he was running out of time. He looked down at his watch to see how much time he had left.

Wait! That's it! That's it! It's time! The answer is time! Measured but not seen, felt but not touched, able to tear down mountains but has no arms! IT'S TIME!

He jumped up and shouted, "I know the answer! I know it! It's time!"

The Sphinx smiled and lowered herself to the ground.

"You have passed the second challenge!" declared Kekrops. The crowd broke into wild cheers and applause.

"VIS-I-TOR! VIS-I-TOR! VIS-I-TOR!" Joey smiled widely and wiped the sweat off his forehead. Even Kekrops was impressed.

"You have done well," the king acknowledged. "You have proven your strength by besting the strongest of our heroes. You have proven your wisdom by outwitting the wisest of our thinkers. But your final task is not an easy one. Your perseverance will be tested as you push Sisyphus' boulder up Mt. Lykavittos."

Say what now?

As Joey left the arena, Xerxes was waiting for him.

"One guess. *Two* men," Xerxes said with a smile.

That evening over dinner, Joey and Xerxes discussed the first two challenges. They laughed about how tiny Joey looked running away from the gargantuan Heracles and Xerxes admitted that he would not have correctly guessed the answer to the Sphinx's riddle.

"Tomorrow you face your final challenge, Joey," said Xerxes sadly.

"I can't wait to get home," Joey said. He thought about the sadness in Xerxes' voice and realized that he would miss Xerxes. "You have been a good friend to me, Xerxes." Xerxes was quiet for a moment then said, "You should get some sleep so you will be rested for your final task."

Mt. Lykavittos looked huge. King Kekrops stood at the base of the mountain. He pointed to a giant boulder beside him.

"You must push this boulder until it reaches the top of Mt. Lykavittos. You have one hour, and if you fail, you will remain in Athens." Kekrops seemed happy at the thought.

Joey stared at the rock in disbelief—it was the size of a small horse and probably weighed twice as much! There was no way a kid could even budge that rock. There was no way an adult could move that rock. Push it all the way up a mountain? Seriously?

"Your time starts… NOW!"

Joey ran to the boulder and started shoving his weight against it with all his might. He strained against it, trying to find a place to grab on. His hands kept slipping and his feet kept sliding out from under him. He kept trying, over and over again, each time with no luck. He started to get mad. He threw himself against the rock again.

Shockingly, as he pushed this time, he felt the boulder begin to move. Encouraged by this, he planted his feet firmly on the ground and pushed as hard as he could. Slowly, the boulder began moving up the hill. He put his

body beneath it and kept pushing and pushing, hoping it wouldn't crush him. As he got closer to the top, the boulder felt like it became heavier and seemed like it got larger. He could feel himself weakening. He tried to fight against it, but he was losing his grip. The boulder came loose, and Joey was barely able to move aside as it rolled out of his grasp and tumbled back down the mountain.

"NO! NO!" Joey cried.

He darted down the mountain after it, but the stone landed right back down where it started. He looked at the rock and felt defeated. There was no way he could push the rock back up the mountain. He sat down.

"Let us help you."

He looked up and saw a crowd of people, around him. The people began to work together to help Joey push the boulder back up the mountain. Joey smiled and thanked them. They pushed and pushed and when the boulder slipped, they worked together to hoist it back up. Slowly, the boulder went higher and higher. With less than five minutes to spare, the crowd helped Joey push the boulder atop the mountain.

Joey hiked back down the mountain and addressed the crowd. "I could never have done this by myself. Thank you all for your help."

Xerxes patted Joey on the back and said, "We are never really alone."

The next morning, the entire city of Athens came to the rock spire to say goodbye to Joey.

Xerxes hugged Joey firmly and with the tiniest of tears in his eyes, said, "I will miss you, my friend."

Joey hugged him back, saying, "Thank you for all your help and your friendship; I will always remember you."

He went to the rock spire and jumped towards it with his eyes closed, hoping he wouldn't slam into it. But he didn't. He passed right through it and into the museum.

Joey felt cool, dry air wash over him. He opened his eyes and saw

harsh, fluorescent light instead of the soft sunlight of Greece. He spun around, discombobulated, and noticed that the revolving door had vanished from the museum, and in its place was a normal door. He felt like he had just stumbled off the Incredicoaster at Disneyland—and that was not an experience he wanted to repeat.

"Well, well, well, if it isn't Bumbler McStumbler," drawled Anthony Giles.

Upon hearing Anthony's voice, Joey felt an urge to cower and run. But he was done running. Joey swiveled around and saw Anthony standing there with all the laughing kids from Joey's class.

I won't let Anthony scare me this time, Joey thought. I beat Heracles. Who's this guy?

"Why do you laugh?" Joey asked, addressing the kids behind Anthony. "He's pushed all of you around before. Why don't you do something about it?"

Mutters came from the crowd of kids behind Anthony.

"I'll help you," said Joey.

"He's right."

"Yeah."

"Who does he think he is? King?"

The other kids moved away from Anthony and fell in line behind Joey. Suddenly, Anthony found himself alone. Joey saw the boy's shoulders slump forward. Behind Anthony, Joey caught a glimpse of a marble figure that looked a lot like Xerxes. He knew he'd never have any trouble from Anthony again.

Maybe being eleven isn't so hard after all.

Using Metaphor

Anna Yang revised her poem, *Picture Perfect*, with mentor, Bronté Bettencourt. Together they focused on using metaphor to highlight the subtext of the poem.

Dear Reader,

Metaphor has an interesting way of appearing in a writer's work. I find that when I set out to write a piece with a particular metaphor in mind that the words come out contrived and didactic. It becomes less organic and more like I'm trying to sound smart, and deep, and complex. Instead, I will write the piece first and then leave it alone for a few days. Only then am I able to glean the subtext beneath the main story's framework.

Anna's piece was brimming with subtext.

In Anna's poem, *Picture Perfect*, the words had so many layers and ideas that it wanted to convey. What was originally a metaphor on writing transformed into a metaphor on music, with a lost narrator who was searching for a greater meaning to her life. With all these branching paths I explained to Anna that she could take the poem in whatever direction she wanted. She could explore the metaphors she laid out to decide what was as the heart of what she wanted to say.

Anna originally thought her changes would focus more on grammar and structure. In actuality she homed in on the musical metaphor. Anna

trimmed the details that she felt would pull the reader's attention away from what she wanted to say. Now, the narrator's search for meaning pertains less to unfinished ideas thanks to changing words like "characters" to "notes", and "sentence" to "symphony" and "song." At the end instead of simply having the character's violin "dangling from her back," Anna changed it to the violin being "a knife to [her] back." Anna's elongated sentence structure and utilization of the musical elements explore both the melodic and harsh notes that a symphony can convey. By focusing on the musical elements, Anna has refined the metaphor in both complexity and depth, allowing it to work on multiple levels.

My advice to you would be to not write a piece with the deeper metaphors in mind. If a metaphor calls to you before you've fully written your piece, be open minded for your writing to surprise you with something more. Get your draft out first before concentrating on the deeper meanings. After completing your draft give yourself a few days before returning to your piece and see what metaphors you can pull from it. Writing has an interesting way of showing us ourselves in ways that we weren't expecting. If you go into the process with a greater meaning set in stone, you're chopping off all the potential paths your piece could take. I suggest getting all the ideas down and then focusing in, versus limiting your piece from the get-go with a single train of thought.

Happy Writing and Draft Without Limits!

Bronté Bettencourt

Bronté Bettencourt graduated from Hamline University with a master's degree of Fine Arts in Writing for Children and Young Adults from Hamline University. This is her third-year mentoring for the Society of Young Inklings Book Contest, which has proven to be both valuable and rewarding in helping young aspiring authors. When she is not writing or working, Bronté is a full time D&D enthusiast, foodie, and YouTube connoisseur. Follow her on Medium and Instagram @elliebronte.

Anna Yang

Anna Yang is a ninth grader at Notre Dame High School. She loves to write, play volleyball, and read mystery and science fiction. She also has a blog (annajyang.wordpress.com) that was started in 5th grade and works on the staff for her school newspaper. She enjoys doing speech, debate, and Model United Nations in her free time.

Bronté Bettencourt: What changed when you revised for metaphor?

Anna Yang: In the beginning of my poem I used the metaphor of a story, but then in the middle I was more emphasizing the music aspect of it. So, after editing I decided to go in and change the overall story to match my music metaphor rather than the writing metaphor.

Q: Where do you like to write?

I like to write outside because it is cooler, and I have nature to describe. It's just inspirational, more inspirational than sitting in my room and looking at the wall.

Q: Did you'd think you'd change so much of your piece?

A: I knew that I was going to make at least some changes, but I think I made changes that are geared toward different aspects rather that I thought it would. I thought I would be working more on grammar and structure, but I actually changed aspects of the plot and that was unexpected.

Q: What advice do you have for other Inklings who don't like revision very much?

A: I think that revision is really useful because often when I look back at my first drafts, they're not really well connected or well planned out as I thought it would be. So, looking back and revising ties the story up and makes it complete.

Q: Are you working on a new piece?

A: Yeah, I'm usually writing, not always like they're not always going to be poetry or stories. Sometimes I just like journaling. I also work for the newspaper for my school, so we also write stories for that. I really like writing, but it doesn't always have to be a creative piece.

Picture Perfect

by

Anna Yang

The train jolts me awake.
Again.
I've lost track of how many
dreams I've left unfinished, how many notes in my head
waiting for the end of a symphony that will
never come.

My fingers reach into my pocket,
touching the roughly cut newspaper article that's supposed to save me.
Well, the young woman in the photo is.

She looks just like me, or as I imagined she would become,
ever since she was taken from my arms
years ago.
Her fingers are long, like mine.
I envision her hands on milky white keys,
thumb on G, pinky on B; the beginning of a melody.
My thinning fingers tap out the song
I learned when I was just a child. I smile slightly, eyes following
the conservatory letters, bright and bold, above her head.

Ghosts of piano notes play in my mind.

I see her eyes, wrinkled like mine, but

from laughing with the children

I think.

I picture little girls with their pleated hair and porcelain

skin like the dolls they carry.

She's much too young to be a mother but

her affection makes me wonder if she is one now.

Young, innocent, naive, as

I had been.

My hands trace along wisps of glimmering hair

loose from a tight blonde ponytail.

I imagine a carefree girl dashing across town

stopping at the corner of a street for a second

before stepping into the bakery. A girl growing up under

the eyes of a loving mother—someone the opposite of her real one, maybe.

Her youthful gaze puts a smile

on everyone's face.

I'm pushed out of my seat as the train lurches to a stop. The man behind me

grumbles

and I step into the crowded aisle. In front of me, cloth of a trench coat ruffles.

Colors dash before my widening eyes. Something in his pocket.

Piano fingers. Delighted eyes. Blonde hair.

I'm not the only one looking for her.

Past the inching line,
through the door, I see the woman. Almost
like the picture. A band of metal
hugs her slender fourth finger. Baby boy tugging
on her skirt. Brown streaks run
through golden hair. Black hourglass case carried
around her shoulders.

I'm at the door now.
Hesitate.

I step onto the platform.

The trench coat
pushes through the crowd. Baby boy
in his arms. Ringed fingers intertwine.
Three silhouettes turning away.
Her Violin is a knife to my back.
Chestnut
highlights grow smaller.
Disappear.

I clench onto the picture.
Again,
I'm left without an ending.
My song
incomplete

The Heart of a Story

Emma Long worked with mentor, Philomena Block, on a revision focused on accentuating the heart of Emma's story, *Lucky Rat.*

Dear Reader,

Stories are powerful because of their long-lasting meaning. When you read a book, you not only follow the journey of the characters. You also discover the true essence of the story. When I met with Emma to revise her story, *Lucky Rat*, we decided to unlock and accentuate **the heart of the story**.

Emma began with a strong story with great details of a rat getting a new home. With this solid base, we first decided to identify the heart of the story. Emma hadn't heard of the "heart of the story" before. I highlighted that its very close to a story's "theme" or "meaning." With this in mind, we tried out a few "hearts" before we found the right one. *Lucky Rat* includes many ideas— moving and experiencing a new place, expressing your feelings, and never forgetting where you come from. Emma had originally written a sentence in the end of her story that summed up never forgetting where you come from. We decided this was a sign, and we worked to build the story to get to that resolution.

In her revision, Emma focused on two techniques in the beginning and middle of the story to develop its heart. First, we added more motivation to

the animal characters around her protagonist, Xiang. Emma did a great job using the setting details to outline the plot points. We added details about the secondary characters, to get a more holistic view of why they treat Xiang the way they do. The other characters' motivation and point of views accentuate the loneliness or happiness Xiang experiences in America and China. Then, we focused on adding more internal dialogue to Xiang. In her original draft, Emma included sections in italics that showed Xiang's inner monologue. This is an effective tool to show contrast between how characters act and speak, versus how they actually feel. I encouraged Emma to add more sections of inner monologue to help the reader understand Xiang's emotional journey from loneliness and uncertainty to acceptance and belonging. These two techniques were used to highlight the heart of the story that you should never forget where you come from.

If you are writing a story, I encourage you to try Emma's approach to incorporating the heart of the story. Reread your story, identify what you want to stand out as the heart of the story, write that down, and see how you can use other characters, and techniques to accentuate that point.

Cheers!

Philomena Block

Philomena Block is an actor, writer, and comedian originally from Santa Cruz, California. Philomena holds two bachelor's degrees—one in musical theatre, the other in psychology— and is trained in playwriting, sketch comedy, and improvisation. Philomena has always been drawn to storytelling and loves developing characters onstage and on the page. Philomena worked as a teacher with the Society of Young Inklings for two years and is so happy to keep supporting young writers with the Inklings Book Contest. When Philomena isn't writing or performing, she works as a marketing professional and loves breathing in the ocean air.

Emma Long

Emma Long is a fifth grader at Woodinville Montessori School. She enjoys gymnastics, collecting stuffed animals and being outdoors. Emma's favorite animal is a Lowland Tapir because they are not very well known by most people and they have hair on their heads that looks like a spike, but she likes all animals. When she grows up she wants to be a scientist.

Philomena Block: Why do you like to write stories? Where do you do most of your writing?
Emma Long: I like to write stories because it's fun to make things up and it can be about whatever you want. I do most of my writing at school.

Q: Can you tell me about how you developed this story?
A: Originally, this was a part of a free writing journal I did in class. I wrote about rats because I like to write about different types of animals. When it came time to enter the Inklings Book Contest, my teacher suggested I use one of my free writing journals. My teacher also encouraged me to write about what I know.

Q: What part of the revision did you think was the most fun to do?
A: I think adding more of the italics and what Xiang was thinking was fun.

Q: What advice would you give young writers who are struggling to revise their work?

A: It is hard to revise your story, because it's already finished. But when you do you can go back and make it even better. You can learn a lot more when you look at it again after a break.

Lucky Rat

by

Emma Long

Faraway in China, close to the southern coast, was an old, rickety, three-story house, with ants crawling through the walls and on the floor.. This was the home for homeless rat children, and it was full of young rats. Among all these young rats, smaller, shyer than the rest, was a rat named Xiang.

One day Xiang was playing upstairs in the playroom with her friends Jade Chen and Min Li. They too were both rats and much more confident than Xiang. Min was seven and Jade was ten. At the foster home, Mrs. Hong was the main caretaker for the rat children.

"Xiang!" yelled Mrs. Hong. "Come here! I have exciting news!"

"Yes Mrs. Hong," replied Xiang in a calm but excited voice as she came downstairs from the playroom.

"Xiang, a family from the United States of America has called to say that they have filled out all of your adoption papers!" said Mrs. Hong, almost more excited than Xiang. "You will be going home tomorrow first thing in the morning."

Later that night at dinner, Min Li asked, "So are you excited about tomorrow?" "I know if I was getting adopted I would be SOOOO excited!"

Min can be so chatty and annoying sometimes, thought Xiang.

"Yeah," said Jade. "No wonder you're the first of the month. Your name means lucky."

I guess Jade doesn't understand either. At least she has more sympathy than Min, Xiang thought to herself.

"I really don't know if I am ready guys," whispered Xiang as she picked nervously at her mostly untouched dinner.

"It is so far away. Everything will be so new and I will miss you guys," Xiang said sadly.

"Well think about this," Jade said, trying to cheer her friend up. "Maybe you will get a better home, without yucky ants, crumbling walls and crammed, partially falling down bunk beds."

Yeah, I guess so, but this is my home and I don't want to go, Xiang thought to herself.

That night Xiang could not sleep. It was dark and cold as the rain pounded on the crowded house. The cold air leaked through the poorly sealed windows. As the wind whipped through the bedroom, it felt like the sky was expressing its sadness with her.

The next day Xiang packed up all her things in a small box covered in green silk from Mrs. Hong. Its contents included a photo of her friends, and necklace with a beautiful, red ruby in the middle from her birth mother. This necklace was the only thing she had left of her after coming to live with Mrs. Hong. Also inside the box was a pair of socks and in her tiny paw she held a smooth, cool, jade stone with "lucky" engraved into it in Chinese. This was a goodbye present from all her friends and Mrs. Hong.

"Ready to go meet your new family?" Mrs. Hong asked.

No, Xiang said to herself, firmly planting that into her head. However, she forced herself to say, "Yes, I think I am."

Then she walked out to the lobby, which was actually a living room made into a lobby, where she saw her parents. Her mother was short, had red, wavy fur with grey and white streaks and seemed welcoming. Her father was quite the opposite. He was very tall, had completely grey fur, and had a stern look with a cross expression as if he wanted to get out of there. In addition, very unlike his wife, he dressed formally, not casually. He looked like a businessman going to a big, important meeting.

"Nihao," said the woman.

"Oh, we can speak English!" laughed Mrs. Hong.

"Okay, is Xiang ready?" the man said impatiently. "I am missing an important meeting!"

"Honey, give Grace some time to say goodbye," Mrs. Miller said laughing a bit. "This is a once in a lifetime chance to have a child!"

Grace? Who is Grace? Is that me? Xiang thought. *I can't believe what I'm doing. I am leaving. Why am I doing this? I said I would never do this!*

"Are you ready, Xiang?" Mrs. Hong asked.

"Yes," Xiang said, trying to sound confident but instead sounding nervous and shy.

"Let's go then," said the impatient man.

"Okay, Mr. and Mrs. Miller," Mrs. Hong said. "Thank you for adopting."

"Xie Xie, Zaijian. I mean thank you and goodbye," Mrs. Miller said.

"Bye, Mrs. Hong," said Xiang.

As they left, Xiang could see Jade peeking around a corner. Her eyes were puffy, red, and had big bags under her eyes from crying and not sleeping and a tear rolled down her cheek.

Poor Jade, this is harder for her than me. Maybe I shouldn't leave. No, No, I can't. Mrs. Hong would be disappointed. Only 2-3 kids are adopted a month. I guess I am kinda lucky, Xiang thought.

The car started. Xiang rolled the window down and waved a little goodbye to her favorite places. The foster home, the pet market with all the little green, yellow and blue parakeets chirping away, the busy streets and the clothing store where she got her shoes when she was little, and finally, the grocery store Mrs. Hong sometimes took the kids to for treats.

She remembered the big pot of eels on the ground, the turtles and frogs in the big nets, and after shopping she got wax apples and sometimes candy. She also knew she would miss the night market that Mrs. Hong always took the little rats to on Chinese New Year with her favorite jiaozi called xiao long bao with the delicious steaming hot soup. As they got to the airport, Xiang looked at the board with the different flights.

A 13-hour flight! That's so long! thought Xiang.

They soon boarded the airplane. Xiang could see her old home. As the plane got higher, she could see her home melt away to where she could only see clouds. After the 13-hour flight, they finally landed in America at midnight. After the long journey from China, they were home. The new house was huge.

"Grace, I mean Xiang, this is your room," Mrs. Miller said happily.

"Thanks Mrs. um—Miller," Xiang said. She was trying to be thankful but her words came out in an unhappy and ungrateful tone.

"Sweetie, please, this is your new home, a new family, a new name— Grace Miller—and a fresh start, so call me Mom, please."

I don't want to call you mom or have a fresh start and I most certainly hate my new name. What kind of name is Grace? Too bad they couldn't have taken Min or Jade too. China was much better.

They got in the car to go to the store. As they passed all the big towers in the city, Grace felt like crying. Everything was so new. The skyscrapers, the new noises, so many people, such a new place!

I will never fit in! Grace thought.

"Tomorrow you will go to school," said Mrs. Miller. "I hope you like it. It's called Forest Wood Elementary. You're in Mr. Thomas's 5th grade class. Also, there is more than just rats; it is an all-animal school."

Huh, Mrs. Hong always taught us at home. I wonder what it is like going to a school.

At dinner, Grace barely picked at her food.

"I think I am going to bed," said Grace as she cleared her plate and went upstairs.

"Honey, do you think Grace is okay?" asked Mrs. Miller in a quiet voice.

"Ah, whatever, she may warm up, eventually," Mr. Miller responded, not even sounding like he cared.

"Okay, you're always right," Mrs. Miller said, still worried.

She still did not agree with her husband.

The next day Mrs. Miller dropped Xiang off at school and said, "Grace, you will have to walk home from school because I am working. Okay?"

Xiang refused to answer. She went to class. Her teacher was Mr. Thomas. He was kind, understanding, and a great teacher.

I hope Mom didn't tell him my story.

In class, Grace sat next to a weasel named Alice, who seemed to like her but acted very weasely—probably because she was a weasel. They worked on math, reading and science. By recess, she had already made a kind of friend in Alice, who wasn't the nicest. Still, Grace was still happier to have a sort of friend rather than none. Grace was shy and not good at making friends so she was surprised that Alice gave her attention. Then at recess, her friend left her.

"Alice, why would you be friends with the new girl? She's a different species for goodness sake!" Alice's friend said.

"Well, she sits next to me in class so I figured I could be nice," Alice said, before running off with her friend. "She is new after all."

As Grace sat on a small bench, a tear trickled down her cheek. Then another. She wiped them off with her sleeve. After school, she slowly walked home.

"Mom!" Grace called.

Where was Mom? She was nowhere.

Grace started panicking. Then the phone rang. It was Mom. She was calling to say she and Dad would be home late.

Right, Mom said she would be home late!

Grace went to her room. She started crying.

I should not be here. I want to go home. My own mother pretends to love me but my father hates me. She does not care. Grace thought about calling the foster home but she did not. *How is this lucky? My name means lucky.*

Then she cried herself to sleep.

The next day Mrs. Miller again drove her to school. Mr. Thomas had assigned a project to work in groups of three. Grace was with Annie, who was also shy and sat in the very back row, and Elise was slightly bossy and sat in the front row and was usually trying to look cool but really wasn't because nobody liked her and she was not the greatest person to be with. Anne was a bunny and Elise was a songbird. Together they worked on the project and managed to get along. Grace and Annie became good friends and it was nice to know Elise too, even if she wasn't liked by the other children and was sort of bossy.

Well, at least I have one friend, Grace thought to herself.

Even though she had a friend, something was still troubling her. First, she wanted to spend more time with her family and second she wanted to see Jade, Min and Mrs. Hong. On Sunday, she suddenly had the courage.

"Mom, will you come home early?" Grace asked.

"Thank you for asking, of course I will," Mrs. Miller said. "But sweetie, you must know your father and I are very busy with work."

The next day Grace came home. To her surprise, both her parents were home early.

"We have a surprise for you, sweetie," Mrs. Miller said.

"Yes, we both stopped work early to take you out to dinner," Mr. Miller said.

"You can choose the restaurant," Mrs. Miller said.

Wow! I can't believe my parents, especially Dad, would come home early! I only asked Mom to come home early, not Dad too. That's even better! So, I guess Dad really does have a soft side.

Grace chose a Chinese restaurant called Dumpling Time.

Now the next question would take more courage.

Finally, she asked, "Mom, can we go back to China? I miss my friends," Grace said.

"I am sorry, sweetie, but your father doesn't want to go back just now," Mrs. Miller said. "He is busy with work because the business he works for isn't doing so well. Sorry."

Grace walked away, slumping, and went upstairs to bed.

Three years later, when Grace was 13, she went back to China. She saw Mrs. Hong and new faces and old faces, and then she saw Min.

"MIN!" screamed Grace.

"Wow, you sound like a whole new person, Xiang," said Min.

"I got a new name! I am now Grace. But you can still call me Xiang," said Grace. "Where's Jade?" asked Grace.

"Jade? You remember her? She left two years ago for the middle of China with her new family," replied Min.

"Do you know what city?" asked Grace hopefully. "Maybe my mom will take me."

"I'm sorry I don't know," Min said in a sad and sympathetic tone. "I haven't seen her in years either."

"I will call her then," Grace said with confidence, while in her head telling herself not to get a silly idea in case it would not work.

"Fine," replied Min, handing Grace a piece of scratch paper with some numbers on it.

"How do you know her number?" Grace questioned.

"She sent a letter to me a year ago," Min said happily.

"Grace, let's go!" Mrs. Miller yelled from downstairs.

"Bye for now," Grace said.

"Goodbye for now. Zaijian," Min said as she took a deep breath.

That night on the airplane ride home, Mrs. Miller asked, "Sweetie, did you have fun visiting your friends?"

"Yeah Mom, I actually did have fun," Grace said, "But Jade wasn't there."

"I am sorry you didn't see her," said Mrs. Miller.

"It's okay, Mom," Grace said. "But can I call her? I am dying to talk to her!" asked Grace.

"Sure sweetie, but when we land." Mrs. Miller said, "The call might mess with the airplane's system and we could crash."

"Okay, when we land."

As the plane got lower, Grace could see all her familiar places. The skyscrapers, the busy streets full of cars and people walking on the side of the road. Everything she used to think was weird and new that she said she would never get used to three years ago. Now Grace called these things familiar.

Then she thought, *Maybe I am meant to be here. After being in America, this feels like my home now. China **and** America.*

When they landed, Grace called Jade. They had a nice conversation. Then finally, Grace felt happiness because she found her place in the world. She knew she was here because people loved her and cared for her.

Huh, this is my home. However, I will never forget China, my friends, Mrs. Hong, everything I love in China. I will never forget my true home and where I actually came from.

She looked down at her necklace she was wearing. It was the one from her mother with the brilliant colored ruby.

"And this," Grace whispered. "Will always remind me."

She was American Grace on the outside but on the inside, she always knew she would be Chinese Xiang.

Character Motivation

Trisha Iyer revised her story, *The Fight for Hope*, with mentor, Melanie Heuiser Hill, focusing on highlighting the motivation that drives her main character.

Dear Reader,

Fleshing out characters is often the work of revision. What is clear to the writer—who the character is, what she wants, what motivates her etc.—sometimes needs a little bolstering for the reader.

We decided to focus Trisha's revision on **character motivation**. She had hints of the main characters' motivations, but they weren't fleshed out. The two of us printed out her story, cut it into identical sections, and worked via Zoom to identify parts that might be shuffled, taken out, or expanded upon. She decided to work on both the ghost's motivation for fighting for civil rights through Olive, and Olive's motivation for doing so as a lawyer. What we discovered was that the traumatic memories of both characters provided excellent motivation for what they do in the story. Through a combination of backstory and memories, the reader now has a better understanding of why the characters of *The Fight For Hope* do what they do.

Here's how Trisha did it: Before revision, both Olive and the ghost had traumatic memories, but they were listed for the reader—told, rather than shown. Trisha worked hard to make those memories come alive in revision. She added whole scenes in some places and in others just a few words to strengthen the backstories and memories of her two main characters. Perhaps most importantly, she gave the same memory to both of them—a newspaper headline and photo—and had each of them experience it in their own way.

I think Trisha might have surprised herself in how dark and frightening some of the memories of her characters turned out to be! But the childhood traumas of her characters is what urged both of them to do what they did in the story.

If you, like Trisha, have a solid plot for your story and you are looking for ways to strengthen that plot, take a look at your characters and get to know them a little better so you can write the why part of what they do.

Happy Writing (& Revising!)

Melanie Heuiser Hill

Melanie Heuiser Hill is the author of the middle grade novel, *Giant Pumpkin Suite*, as well as the picture book, *Around The Table That Grandad Built*, both published by Candlewick Press. She has an MFA in Writing for Children and Young Adults from Hamline University. Melanie lives, reads, and write with her family in Minneapolis, MN. She is currently working on two middle grade novels, as well as a small handful of picture books.

Trisha Iyer

Trisha Iyer is a young writer who has loved reading since she picked up her first Berenstain Bears picture book at age four. As she grew older, this passion for reading prompted her development into a writer who keenly observes and comments on the world around her in her stories and poems. Trisha currently attends 8th grade at the Harker Middle School, where she pursues her passions of following current events, studying the history and culture of Ancient Rome, and eating chocolate. As part of a school trip to Washington, DC earlier this year, she visited the Supreme Court's courthouse and was in awe of how so much history has been made through the landmark court decisions delivered in that room. Her experience led her to write The Fight for Hope, which explores how to fight for justice in an alternate history setting in which Brown v. Board of Education ruled against Brown, keeping Jim Crowism alive in America.

Melanie Heuiser Hill: What changed when you revised for character motivation?

Trisha Iyer: The first draft of this story focused primarily on the ghost and how he/she, desperate for a desegregated America, encouraged and frankly pushed lawyer Olive Randall into successfully arguing for civil rights in her side of the Supreme Court case occurring in the story. As a result, when writing this draft, I only viewed Olive as a pawn of the ghost who carried out its wishes through her.

However, while revising, I realized that I needed to flesh out the ghost's motivation for fighting for civil rights; in addition, Olive needed more of a backstory to explain why she would choose to argue a civil rights case that could overturn everything her father, who had successfully argued for segregation

and the Board of Education's cause in 1954, had worked for. Through revising for character motivation added Olive's memories of her traumatic childhood to the story; I also revisited and expanded upon the ghost's memories of life in the 1950s, adding more details and small storylines to what was originally a laundry list of injustices (such as segregated water fountains, dining venues, and so on).

Q: What are you most proud of in the revisions you made?

A: I am extremely proud of the storyline I gave Olive, in which I explore her motivations for fighting for civil rights and her backstory through memories. I had to think outside the box to come up with reasons for why Olive wants to defy her father so badly, and I eventually created for her an extremely traumatic relationship with her father, who is not only a blatant racist but also a vindictive man who emotionally abuses Olive. Some of the more painful memories, such as when Olive must abandon her dog Corky and when she attends her father's funeral, forced me to write a truly cruel character and express some very strong and negative emotions (which I have never experienced so deeply myself) on the page. I'm a very cheerful person, so expressing such hatred and cruelty in words pushed me as a writer, and I'm incredibly happy with how beautifully the scenes turned out.

Q: What advice do you have for writers who don't like the task of revision?

A: Revision does not have to be a long and arduous process. Revising a piece might give the impression that it's not satisfactory, even after a writer has put in hours of work to perfect the draft, and therefore can seem like a daunting quest to "make it good." However, revising can be a truly enjoyable task, where you get to explore the world created in your piece and play with the plot. Sit down for a short period of time (say, an hour) and hash out your revisions—as

in, get it over with! Whether you need to cut down your existing draft or make additions, do it for an uninterrupted period of time without second-guessing yourself. Work in a nice spot that energizes you (I like working on a sunny bench in my backyard) and most definitely do your first pass by hand—if cutting, print out your story and make cross-outs with a marker, and if adding material, write it out by hand. There's something comforting about holding your creation in your hands, and it makes your task of revising more concrete and manageable.

Q: What do you enjoy most about the writing process?

A: My favorite part of the writing process is outlining my story or poem; this stage takes place after I've received the idea—what I call the "spark"—for it and before the actual writing of the draft. This is the part where I make my outline (I am a great fan of outlines) and flesh out the details of the story, creating my different characters, working out all of the details of the plot and how to connect them to each other smoothly, and consider where and when to add symbolism. This is the real meat of the story—the laying out of the skeleton and muscle and organs in careful array, while writing the actual draft is only the actual zap of life to fully form the piece and bring it to life. This is the part where I allow my imagination to go crazy as I expand the premise of the work (the original idea) into a working outline.

Q: Are you working on a new story?

A: Yes. It is still in the earliest stages of development, but it echoes and exaggerates the stress of today's college applications. The story is set in a dystopian world where all teenagers have an app that tells them whether they are "enough" to get into the top university in the nation, and the protagonist finally snaps under the pressure, leading to adverse consequences for her life and her world.

The Fight for Hope

by

Trisha Iyer

The best time of year.

Autumn is just beginning to cede its territory to winter, but clutches at its last few days with desperate hands. White mist and hazy fog snakes through the streets of Washington, DC, while the skies open and pour out all the rain that the clouds have saved up carefully all through summer, drop by drop. Gloomy clouds dance at the window of the Supreme Court's courtroom.

The moisture is sucked up eagerly by you, your only sustenance as you lay in the shadows of the velvet drapes . . .

. . . waiting . . .

And finally she comes. Shrewd eyes rove about while the rest of her stays still. Sitting primly on the bench, she takes furious notes about the case unfolding in front of her, prepares her own arguments—which, you know, she will give in a few days' time. Her brain is pulsing with ideas, you can feel it . . . taste it . . . you are excited now, roused in a way you have not been in fifty years . . .

For she is a very good lawyer. Perhaps the best.

You decide to swirl down into her as she sits there, try to get a read on her. Leaching into her pores, you sneak up into her brain and poke around, testing the firmness of the gray matter. You skim your eyes over her memories, see her face as a toddler, teenager, all the way up to adult.

You learn her name: Olive Randall.

You see her mother and brothers, then push on, probing her frontal lobe until a strong memory draws you in—the memory of her dog Corky's comforting smell of pollen and fresh dirt. You find that Corky, an unfortunately named yet inexplicably adorable black and brown terrier, was Olive's first pet. All of her friends in junior high had begun to sport small pedigree poodles dangling out of their glossy purses, as was the fad, but Olive had Corky instead. She had found him one night in the alley behind her house, munching on discarded scraps of steak from Sunday dinner, and she fell instantly in love with his soft, understanding brown eyes. Olive had asked her father to keep Corky on one of his better days, when he discussed school with Olive over the dinner table and ruffled her curls with gentle fingers—and he agreed to take in Corky, so long, he cautioned with a jovial wink, as she kept her grades up.

A new memory, carrying the heady magnolia and vanilla scent indicating that it is newly-formed, engulfs you. You see Olive standing erect, sweating out of a black peacoat—she had flown directly out of Massachusetts, where she was completing her last year of law school, for the funeral and had forgotten to dress for the milder Southern winter weather. Her mother pushes her forward, admonishing, "Say goodbye to your father"—but instead, Olive merely stared at Charles' pale, silent grave and read the epitaph:

Here lies Charles "Chuck" Randall

Wise, tenacious, and ever willing

To champion Whites' Rights.

Olive noted that the grave did not describe him as kind—she supposed that it was wrong to lie on something as permanent as a gravestone. Olive had still been in elementary school when, one morning, found that the newspaper lying on the kitchen table had her father's face splashed across the front. In blaring block letters, the headline proclaimed him to be a hero lawyer, having won the Supreme Court case of the century. Her father was smiling in the photo, and the rare sight sat uneasily in her stomach, giving her indigestion as she gulped down Cheerios—even at a young age, Olive couldn't quite swallow around the idea of him as a hero.

Now, older and wiser, she knew that Chuck was not a benevolent champion, but rather a would-be sculptor, pushing African-Americans to the very bottom of the social ladder, forcing young Olive into the stifling mold of the perfect daughter, trying to play God with the entire world—and the worst part: he was successful. As Olive bowed her head in front of the grave and stepped back into the huddle of her remaining family, Olive's resolve hardened. If her father so badly wanted her to be a lawyer, she would become one—and outshine Chuck Randall.

A glimmer of admiration glows in your chest, a warm fist holding fast to the promise of this woman. But how steely is her resolve to follow through on this case? You still know so little about Olive; these fragments of her childhood, these troubled little vignettes, cannot alone speak for her belief in your cause.

Your foraging fingers pause thoughtfully at the trembling, spongy section devoted to her father (the largest part): tense with worry and near her amygdala, it presses into the headache-pinched nerves of her forehead. She does not like him: as a hazy white memory floats up and presents itself to you, you see a young Olive coming home from school with a report card pinched between two fingers. On the bus, she, like her fellow seventh-graders, had tilted the yellow paste envelope toward the glare of the sun and hoped that the

letters would shine through—and they did, but they danced and squirmed and rearranged themselves on the page, impossible to read.

When Charles saw the report card, he stood slowly and took off his belt, twisting it viciously in his hands.

"You think this is funny, Olive?" he shouted, his face flushing as red as the savagely-inked C in Language Arts on her report card. "All the colored children your age read and write well, and they sit in a one-room schoolhouse every day! Yet you won't be better than them, you, you *refuse* your birthright as a superior to them!"

At first, her father tried to make Olive throw out Corky herself, but she curled up in the safe corner of her bookshelves and turned her face to the wall—the lack of eye contact made her defiance easier to carry through. Charles soon lost patience and seized Corky himself; wrapping fingers under the wriggling dog's forelegs in a painful grip, he disappeared into the alley behind the house, returning Corky to the place he had first come from. Swallowing tears—Charles hated weakness—Olive locked away Corky's bed, with the tufts of brown fur clinging to it, and all of his chew toys, some of which still glistened with his saliva. As Olive turned the key, the cold metal biting into her fingers, she glanced down at the items one last time. But she only saw his tiny face with the soft, sweet eyes, confused and expecting Olive to at any moment scoop him up and return him to his place nestled in bed—

You jerk out of this memory, your breath coming in harsh, ragged gasps. An unwanted tear of empathy drops from your eye. Then you plunge even deeper into her brain, to seek more of Olive Randall's experiences with her father, daring yourself to manage the pain . . .

You cannot. Shrieking at his horrid face, you whirl away from her, down and out of her nostrils (now flaring with confusion), and flee back to the safety of the velvet drapes, where you are above worldly problems. Yet you

cannot forget what you have seen. His presence follows you as you curl back up in the shadows of the curtains, clenching your hands, as you stare with unseeing eyes at the chairs of the nine great Justices.

You stare at the podium, where he argued his case decades ago, and won . . .

Sentencing *you* . . .

You will make her understand. You will make her see. You must. For there is always a second chance, even for you . . . even after death . . .

You laugh hollowly. The whispering noise spreads down the spine of everyone in the courtroom, makes the Chief Justice shift uncomfortably in her chair. *Even after death.*

You summon your courage again, nurse it back to full health. You enter her brain once again.

You see her thoughts, the whirlwind thoughts of a turbulent mind. It boils over with words, but at the core, you find the hard truth.

She is giving up. She is backing out of her case. She has no arguments for it, you hear her telling herself, the excuse ringing weak in her ears. She is afraid—of not having anything to say in front of the highest court in the country, but also of what her father might think, if he could see her now, fighting for a cause he regarded with such disdain. For all of her determination in erasing his legacy, she is still a six-year-old girl again, begging her father to look at her lovingly, instead of as a mistake that must be corrected, as he twists his belt in his hands.

No . . . You whisper to yourself, panicking. You squeeze your ghostly

eyes in frustration and thrust your spectral hands deep into her brain. Shoving your own memories—buried-deep-down memories, locked-in-the-ugly-sock-drawer memories—into her eyes and brain, you transport her to your own childhood.

Of living in the 1950s . . . of eating on flimsy paper trays with plastic cutlery on the back steps of the restaurant while you peeked inside the building, watching others eat the same meal—the best casserole a quarter could buy in town—off of china plates (with blue painted decorations around the rims) and sit in shiny leather booths, the very picture of happy families.

Of having to share the same sorry metal cup-shaped excuse for a water fountain after a tiring recess game, when the sun glared down on your dark brow and made you thirst for water.

Far from pristine, the rusty metal fountain was crusted with mold that gave the water the same dissatisfying flavor as your sweat-soaked gym socks. Of how your friends saved up every penny to buy your way into a good seat in the theater and show you a good time. For a few moments, the usher's stern expression wavered as he stared at the money, and you began to dream of plush velvet cushions with padded armrests, where you would not have to crane your scrawny neck to see the pictures on the silver screen. The image of his greedy fingers snatching up your friends' carefully scrounged-up funds before he escorted you with a sardonic smirk to the very last row of wooden benches, with the very worst view, burns bright and harsh, like fluorescent lighting, in your mind. Still you show her more memories:

Of being sneered at and being called names, degrading names that demoted you from the human being that you knew you were, to the near-worthless waste of space that they saw through their piggy, bigoted eyes. You show this poor little lawyer girl what Jim Crow's fat thumbs feel like, pressing you down, closing his hands around your throat while you struggle for air . . .

Air—that is, the one gasp of humanity you needed to stay alive. There was a hope of it coming back in 1954, when African-Americans were finally standing up for their rights, suing for the ability to be integrated and equal instead of separate. And her father argued for the segregated school districts, and he was very good at his job. Too good. So good that he won the case, keeping separate but equal alive. The Board of Education won the case, and being Brown—all over, from the roots of your hair to the soft flesh between your toes—continued to connote inferiority.

One chance for air . . . yet the hope was snatched away. You remember walking to your school, the same dingy room that had housed you since kindergarten and would continue to house you until you dropped out to work in the fields, and seeing a child your age hawking newspapers from a small cart. He had tilted his newsboy cap to you and waved a headline tantalizingly in your direction, a part of the same barter-dance you two had conducted for ages now. But instead of politely refusing as usual, the block letters of the headline sizzled, black and sinister, on the page, proclaiming Charles Randall the hero of the century for—for winning the case against you. That night, his inked photograph floated loftily in the darkness as you closed your eyes; his self-righteous smirk and his pale, twisting eyebrows haunted you. You rose with the sun the next day, but while the sun was as cheerful as ever, you were not—savage bitterness crept into your soul, and the hopeful, optimistic child part of you, bright like the sun, was smashed forever by the hammer of Charles Randall's searing words, wicked mouth, traumatizing face.

Over time, the bite of the cruelty has faded into a numb ache, yet it is still there, gnawing away at you and your people, who have been allowed more hygienic water fountains but are still herded into squalid schools where there is not a single blond head or fair face in sight.

From deep within Olive's consciousness, you hear the faint sounds of

the external world raging like a storm, see the signs of life in the present world above. Lightning crackles at the window, waving at you with yellow fingers. Thunder drums into a dull, meaningless roar. You hear your own ragged breathing, unstable. Just like your mind. It is time to go, you realize. There is nothing more you can do to alter the world of the living when you are so far removed, yet so attached to it.

You leave. Slowly, reluctantly, you leave. You can only hope she will understand.

You retract your fingers one by one from her skull and float back to your velvet nest. All you can do is cross your translucent fingers and hope. You dare to hope one more time.

Two days later, you watch from your perch on the frieze above the Justices' chairs. You reach out your fingers and sense other ghosts, who have suffered as much as you have, emerging from their enclaves inside the carved faces on the frieze. Hope vibrates within them and reaches you, warming the cavity where your heart was.

Olive Randall stands at the podium, fidgeting with the hem of her blazer. Her fingers are nervous, but her face is set, determined. The nine Justices float into the room through a red curtain, those omnipotent beings holding the reins of fate in their hands once again.

Olive speaks. The thirty minutes allotted to her are fleeting, and her words paint pictures of misery, oppression, injustice—they share your story. Although Olive was once at a loss for words, they pour from her lips now, fighting for a chance to show the Justices why civil rights are needed in this

country. The clock flashes a warning red as she nears her time limit, and Olive delivers a final plea:

"Civil rights are merely two small words, yet they hide stories—entire lives—behind them. Integrated *and* equal: three equally small words, yet they represent the possibility of a better America. An America that can be created through Your Honors' decision to support our side."

You sigh, nodding in agreement: her words have become your entire afterlife's mission.

And then she is done. Waiting is agony, but time is a trifle to you, who have waited so long already. But finally, months later, on a bright April morning, the Justices make a unanimous decision. For Olive's side. *For you.*

The sun breaks through, and the clouds carry all you ghosts up to heaven, to your eternal peace.

A Satisfying Ending

Suhani Gupta worked with mentor, Malar Ganapathiappan, on a revision focused on tying up the final knot at the end of Suhani's story, *One Small Light.*

Dear Reader,

Imagine a central thread passing through a sewing piece. At the end, a knot signifies completion, connecting the beginning to the end.

Tying this knot at the end of a story can be tricky. Sometimes endings feel too abrupt. How do you touch upon the main character's conflict and address it in the ending to give the reader a sense of completion? This is what Suhani and I worked on in the revision.

Suhani's original ending followed the climax with an abstract concept distinct from the rest of the story's wonderfully relatable and realistic interactions.

In order to give the ending more **satisfying closure**, Suhani took a few steps. First, she developed her metaphor and added subtle details through the story. Second, she considered the characters and tone. She tweaked the dialogue to better match the characters and give the main character a more active role. Finally, she modified the

beginning of the story to touch on an element of the ending.

The key to Suhani's revision for a satisfying ending was consistency. Consistency of the theme through the story as well as the characters' interactions with each other.

If you are struggling with your ending, try answering these questions:

- What feeling do you want to leave the reader with?
- How can you address the main character's goals or conflicts in the ending?
- Do the beginning, middle, and end connect?

If you're stuck, take a look at what is introduced in the beginning and see if you can connect the ending to the same ideas. Don't force the ending; allow your main character to carry the central thread through.

Good luck!

Happy writing,

Malar Ganapathiappan

Malar Ganapathiappan is a writer, Inklings writing mentor, writing coach, and member of the Society of Children's Book Writers and Illustrators. She holds a bachelor's degree in Psychology. Sharing inspiration, creativity, and perspective through stories gives her joy. When not reading or writing, she enjoys nature, fitness, energy work, art, and animals.

Suhani Gupta

Suhani Gupta is a sixth grader at The Harker School. She loves to read and also enjoys listening to music. Although she may seem shy at first, her friends describe her as energetic and funny. She has only started to write very recently, but already knows that she wants to do something related to it when she is older.

Malar Ganapathiappan: What do you enjoy about writing?

Suhani Gupta: I have a lot of ideas. I love reading, and whenever I read a book, I always try to make up my own characters and see how they would fit inside the novel. One day my friend and I wrote a story and I thought it was really interesting to see how the characters I came up interacted with the storyline we came up with. My favorite part of writing is writing the ending and the beginning.

Q: How did you get the idea for this story?

A: I don't know where I got the story—it just popped into my head. At first, I was going to do a girl and her sister with AIDS, but it's hard to cure someone with AIDS. After I ruled out AIDS, cancer was probably the next best thing to do because I know more about cancer. I chose leukemia because some of my family members have had leukemia and recovered.

Q: How did your story change after your revisions for creating a satisfying ending?

A: The light metaphor became more developed and the ending changed. The storyline didn't change at all. The changes to the ending made it more consistent with the rest of the story. That makes the reader less surprised by any sudden changes.

Q: What are your favorite books?

A: *Warcross*. I also like the *Hunger Games* and *The Kingdom of Back*.

Q: Do you ever feel blocked?

A: Yeah, definitely. Sometimes when I'm trying to come up with a storyline, I get blocked. I take a break, play games, read, and then go back to the story and try to come up with ideas. I think sometimes I just need to clear my mind.

One Small Light

by

Suhani Gupta

The light on the ceiling in the waiting room shined directly on my eyes, making me wince. Of course I was in the one seat that had the stupid light shining on my face. I looked around for another place to sit, but there was none.

Ugh, hospitals are so annoying.

I could almost hear Lynn's voice in my head. *Don't be so negative, Isa.* I had to calm down. *Breathe in, breathe out.*

An hour ago

"Isa! Why are you looking at memes? You should be doing your homework!"

I sighed and looked up. "Okay, Mother Lynn. Don't get ahead of your age."

My sister swatted me on the head. "I have to go to the doctor today. Wanna come?"

"Yeah, sure, 'cause I *always* want to go to the doctor with you to talk about fun leukemia stuff!"

"No need to be so huffy."

"You do realize you were just telling me to do my homework and then you asked me to go to the hospital with you?"

"Isa, please. I'm really stressed. I have to balance my illness and the chemotherapy and school and everything… remember that long stretch of time when I couldn't even go to school? Because of 'leukemia stuff'?"

"Fine! You make me feel so bad. But please, can Ethan not come? He ruins everything."

"Did I say I was going to ask him? And you really should be nicer to your younger brother."

"Yeah, yeah, whatever."

I followed Lynn to her car, sighing. I hated when my sister took me with her to the doctor. I didn't want to hear her and Dr. Talia talk about her illness. I didn't want to know about the death statistics from leukemia. But I couldn't say no sometimes.

Lynn blasted her K-pop music in the car, jarring my thoughts.

"Ahh! My ears are bleeding! Turn it off! Turn it off! Please!"

She cranked up the volume a little more. "Serves you right."

We finally reached the hospital, and Lynn had to turn her K-pop off. I sighed with relief.

I dutifully followed her out of the car and into the hospital. I really wanted all this cancer stuff to end. Maybe because ever since Lynn got leukemia, Mom and Dad completely ignored me. Ethan was still fine, being the youngest and naughtiest. So I wanted attention. Even though I knew I wasn't supposed to. Even though Lynn deserved it.

I sat on the boring gray stools inside Dr. Talia's room with Lynn, waiting for her to come.

I sighed and bunched up my knees. I wished that I hadn't let Lynn force me to come. My stomach felt queasy, even though I hadn't eaten anything.

"Can I go, please?" I asked my sister. "I don't feel so good."

"I'm not driving you all the way home now. You should have said something before."

"Please?"

"Fine, you can wait outside and walk around a little bit."

"All right."

And now here I was, circling the waiting room and trying to block out my thoughts. *What if something happened to Lynn? What if she... died?*

I kicked myself and tried to stop thinking about my sister. *Deep breaths. Deep breaths.*

Gradually, my heart rate slowed and I felt calm again. *Lynn is not going to die.*

I lay in bed, listening to the faint *ding ding ding* of my alarm. *Ugh. It's Monday.*

Thoughts of Lynn immediately rushed into my head. *Where is she?* I wrestled with my covers and sat up. *Where is Lynn?*

And then I realized that she was in her room, still sleeping. I sighed in relief and stood up, one foot at a time.

As soon as I got out of bed, I had this strange feeling. And not a good one. But still, I ignored it and instead focused on getting myself ready.

That was a mistake.

My friend, Alyssa, ran up to me.

I half-smiled. "Hi. What took you so long?"

"Mr. Chen was being soooo annoying, okay! Ya know, he was just talking and droning on, ya know, and everyone was laughing like it was funny even though we were wasting time and all I did was watch the clock but then I realized it was broken, so... That reminds me the bell today was so quiet, ya know, what's wrong with the office people? And a lot of people were late today to P.E. What if they're planning a rebellion against running the mile or something? I'm probably gonna pretend to hurt myself, so I don't have to run it. Also, did you know Mrs. Jackson broke her leg? Now we have a sub for English. It's so sad! I like Mrs. Jackson. But I think she hates me because I suck at English. Also I probably annoy her by being such a suck up. Anyway, the musical auditions are coming up, ya know, and I'm auditioning, but I probably won't get it so yeah, but we get hot Cheetos after the performance."

The corners of my lips turned up. "Okay, okay, great. Enough info. Where's Emi?"

"Boo!"

I tilted my head upward and smiled at my best friend, Emika. "Lyss was rambling, Emi. Can you make her go away?"

"Yeah, but I was planning on rambling too, so..."

"Oh, no. Please don't."

"Fine. Then... let's change the subject. How's your sister?"

Worst subject change ever. I leaned on her shoulder. "Can we not talk about this? For some weird reason I feel like something bad is going to happen to her."

"Just keep really careful and she'll be fine I think."

Lyss immediately jumped into the conversation. "Oh my god, Isabelle, I was being so insensitive about your sister! I didn't even ask about her! I am *so, so, so* sorry! I didn't mean to make you feel bad at *all*! Please forgive me!"

Sighing, I replied, "It's okay. I know you like talking."

"Still, I'm *so* sorry!"

"Anyway, Emi, you were going to say something right?" I asked, changing the subject.

"Oh yeah! Yesterday in Costco, there was this girl..."

I tuned out her words. *Nothing will happen. Nothing.*

Nothing.

Finally, after a long, long morning of classes and thinking about Lynn, it was time for lunch. It was Ella's birthday today. And if Emi was my best friend, then Ella was practically my sister. I smiled and skipped along to the door of my math classroom.

When I got outside, the sun beat down straight on my head. I wanted to scream at it to stop, but I refrained from doing that. *What is it with me and stupid blinding light?*

I decided to ignore the sun and instead walked along the path to the lunch tables. Ella would love the gift I was going to give her.

All of a sudden, my friend Adler walked up to me. He was carrying a huge shiny, deep blue bag.

"Hi, Isabelle," he said.

"Hey. Is the bag for Ella?"

"Yeah. I have a question, though. You've been friends with her longer, right? So... uh... do you think she would like a... um... a book? *Warcross*, I mean. Like, Emi's favorite. But not for Emi, I mean, I got it for Ella. And a new Oxi-gel, because her wood pencils always make squeaky sounds. And also I got her a purse, but not really a purse, because it doesn't really..."

"No, Adler. She wouldn't like that at all," I replied, barely containing my smile.

"Oh! I mean, it's not that I got her all that stuff... but I sorta did. Well, I mean..."

"You've said 'I mean' four times in the last few minutes. And you and Ella? Aww! I totally ship you!" I clasped my hands together in a heart. "Don't worry, I bet she'll love it. You're so cute together!"

He rolled his eyes at me. "Seriously? You made me have high blood pressure!"

"Oh no! I don't want you to explode in front of Ella!" I replied sarcastically.

"Shut up. I shouldn't have come to you."

"I'm totally telling Ella!"

"If you tell Ella, I'm going to scream all your crushes to the whole school."

"I swear, if you scream my crushes to the school I'm gonna rip your head off and flush it down the toilet. In the girls bathroom," I replied, matter-of-factly. "But I guess it's fine because she'll guess that you like her. She's not as clueless as you."

"Hey! What's that supposed to mean!?"

He ran after me as I started to walk away, a huge grin on my face.

"Do you really think she'll like it?"

"Yes! Now go give it to her." I pushed him towards our lunch table.

When he saw Ella, his face flushed. "Oh. Hi. I just have this..." He made a wide gesture towards the bag. "It's not that much. Well, I guess it kind of is. Oh, never mind. I hope you like it, though."

Ella looked up from her drawing, her cheeks turning pink. "Um... thanks? I mean, I really like it. Thanks so much." She half-hugged him awkwardly. "What do you have for me, Isa?" she asked, changing the subject quickly.

I gave her a small bag. "I know, I know, nothing as fancy as Adler, but I guarantee you'll like it."

"So mysterious." She peeked inside the bag and took out the duck stuffed animal that I had messily packed inside with yellow wrapping paper.

"OMG!!! It's a DUCKIE!!!" she yelled, hugging me. And not an awkward one like Adler's.

Suddenly, someone ran up behind us, ruining the moment. "Happy birthday to you!"

Emika, Cameron, Liam, and Lyss chorused, painfully off-tune. I wasn't surprised that Emi's voice rang louder than everyone else's.

Everyone was staring at us. Ella hid under the duck that I gave her. Out of the blue, a random person yelled, "Happy birthday, Ella!"

Emi smiled and waved. "Ella says thanks!"

"Ugh, I wish I didn't have any friends," Ella groaned, embarrassed. "Can we just endure the rest of lunch in silence?"

"Yeah, guys," I said, rolling my eyes. "Enough noise pollution."

As soon as I had finished saying that, someone tapped me on the shoulder. I looked behind me, realizing that it was the principal. *Why was he here?*

"Isabelle, I would like you to come to my office," he said, stiffly. I froze up. *What had I done wrong?*

Either way, I quickly followed. Soon, we reached his office. I sagged against a chair, still scared.

"I'm sorry, Isabelle, but I have bad news. Your sister has been rushed to the hospital. Do not panic, she went immediately into treatment. I'm sure she will be fine. Your mother is calling you to go home to process this information. I sincerely hope that your sister is okay."

My ears stopped hearing after he said the word, "hospital." I made a

disgruntled sound my mouth not able to function properly.

"Your mother is waiting for you at the back loading zone." He led me to the door of the office.

Lynn was in the hospital. Lynn was in the hospital. Lynn was in the hospital. Not just for a checkup. Something was happening. No, no, no no no.

In the car, Mom and Dad were trying to reassure my brother that Lynn would be okay. And failing. We were driving to the hospital... or were we driving home? I didn't know. My vision was foggy and obscured by tears, and my hands were balled in fists. I couldn't hear, couldn't see, couldn't feel.

Even Ethan stopped ranting long enough to ask, "Isa, are you okay?"

Which I obviously wasn't.

The next day, when I sat at our table, still sort of in shock, I noticed obvious tension in the air between the boys and the girls.

"What's wrong?" I asked Emi.

She sighed and rolled her eyes. "Ella will tell you."

"Ella, what's wrong?"

"Lyss will tell you," Ella replied quietly, looking down at the table.

I ground my teeth together. "No," I said. "*You* will tell me, because I am asking you. What's wrong?"

"Yesterday, Liam went to the office because he got in trouble and then he got really mad at everyone, I don't even know why. And then Lyss yelled at him. And Liam got more mad, and she accused him of keeping secrets, and then... you weren't there to be peacemaker and everyone got really mad." Ella

looked back down at the table, going back to whatever she was sketching.

"And now we all kind of want you to sort all this out."

Nobody cared. Nobody even cared that Lynn was in the hospital. All they cared about were their own stupid problems. Nobody even asked me about Lynn. And now they were all mad at each other because they got in a stupid fight. And they expected me to fix it.

I crossed my arms over my chest. "I'm not fixing this. Figure it out yourselves. And I am not going to pick sides, no matter what. Don't you dare make me do that."

The rest of lunch, though, passed in mostly silence with me trying to talk to my friends, trying to make them friends again. I guess that I couldn't stop being a peacemaker, even when I wanted to. It took my mind off things. At least for a little while.

I was at the hospital. Yet again. Sitting by Lynn's side. I was missing school today. I couldn't leave Lynn.

She smiled up at me. "Don't worry, Isa, I'll get better. Of course I will."

"Yeah—it's just..." *It was too fast. Too fast. I wasn't prepared, Lynn wasn't prepared, we all couldn't keep up. It was going way too fast.*

Lynn pulled me in for a hug. "I will be *fine*. Now go. Focus on your school stuff."

I took a deep breath. "Okay. Bye. See you."

"Love you! Bye."

With a heavy heart, I trudged to our car and sat in it with Mom. We

passed the drive in silence, both of us thinking about my sister. Both of us crossing our fingers that nothing too bad would happen.

When we got home, I felt my phone buzz. I picked it up, wondering who was texting me. It was a text from Emika.

what happened, isabelle?

where r u?

we need to talk

And from Ella.

isa, r u ok?

I sighed and texted back:

emi's right.

we need to talk.

i'll tell my mom where i'm going and

meet u outside.

"Mom, I'm going out!" I yelled.

"Okay, but come back quickly!"

"Yeah! It's just to meet Ella and Emika."

"Remember to wear a jacket!"

I shrugged on a jacket and headed outside into the chilly fall air.

Emi and Ella waved to me, and I walked over to them.

"Isa, what's wrong?" Ella asked. "You're so out of it these days. And you're missing school! I honestly thought that you would get worked up over the boys and girls fighting thing. Did something happen?"

"It's about Lynn." I shivered, barely able to feel my mouth making the words. "She went to the hospital because of her cancer, and I'm not talking about this anymore!"

I kicked a rock and sent it scattering against the hard concrete.

"Lynn is in the hospital?!" Emi said.

Hearing it from her mouth made it worse.

"Yeah."

They both enveloped me in hugs. "We're so sorry, Isabelle. It's gonna be okay."

I cried into their arms.

It was going to be okay.

Lynn's condition had gotten much worse over the past few days. Even though she had medical treatment. All my friends were super understanding, but... I was missing school again today.

Can't wait for all the makeup work when I get back! I thought, sarcastically.

It didn't matter to me though. Not if Lynn was gonna *die*. The word made me shiver. Mom said that today was when we found out if Lynn was going to be okay or not. Everyone said that she was going to be okay. Except for the doctor, who said that she had very little chance of pulling through. *Stupid doctor.*

Today was a beautiful day, all sunny and bright after all the days of rain we had before. But now night fell, taking all the happiness with it. I even saw some dumb kids playing with lanterns outside. Idiots. They were so full of hope, even though there was nothing to be hopeful about.

I sat on the bench, rocking back and forth. *She had to be okay.*

But the odds were never in my favor. Or her's, for that matter. *Sorry, Effie Trinket.*

Suddenly the door opened and the doctor came out. I crossed my fingers under the chair.

Maybe she wouldn't die.

"I'm sorry," the doctor said, "But there's not much hope. There's a 98% chance that Lynn won't be able to come out of this alive. It's a lost cause. I'm very sorry."

"What? That can't be true! No way! You're wrong! She can't just die like that!" Ethan yelled. People started staring at us. "She wouldn't just leave like that."

"It's okay, Ethan," Mom said, tiredly, looking devastated.

No. No. It isn't okay. It really isn't.

"I'm going! I'm going to see her!" Ethan said.

"Stop it," I whispered. "Please. Just let nature take its course."

"So you're just gonna sit there?" Ethan demanded.

"Yes, okay? Yes! I'm just gonna stay here. You can go see Lynn die if you want to," I said.

Ethan finally seemed to register the news. Silent tears streamed down his face as he sat back down on the chair.

"You *can* go see her if you want to," the doctor said. I hadn't realized he was still here through Ethan's episode.

I really couldn't resist. I rose up and followed the doctor, my feet dragging on the ground.

Ethan followed me, trying to wipe his tears away. Mom and Dad still sat there, staring at the wall.

I tried to ignore the fact that she was dying when I saw Lynn in the hospital bed. I sat on one side of the bed, holding her hand, ignoring the doctor's warnings.

When was the last time I saw her eyes open? What was the last thing I said to her? Would she remember me? Did she know I was here? Did she know that there were people here—her family—who loved her and wanted her to fight? Had she lost hope already?

Ethan copied me and sat on her other side, sniffling. "Don't go," he whimpered. "Please."

We sat with her for a while, my brother crying the whole time and me just barely holding in together.

I felt a small squeeze on my hand. It was so soft, so subtle, I almost thought that I imagined it. But then it came again, harder and more steady.

"Lynn! Lynn!" I said, unable to control myself.

"What?" Ethan asked.

"Lynn! Are you there? Are you really there?"

The doctor came up behind us. "What happened?"

"She squeezed my hand!"

"Really?"

"Yes! I felt it! I really did."

She was there. Somewhere, she was there.

Ethan and I sat in the room for a few more minutes, calling her name at periodic intervals.

Finally, he said, dejectedly, "Isa, I think you might have imagined her squeezing your hand. Or even if you didn't, maybe she... passed right after you felt her. Or something. But I don't think she'll wake up now."

"Shut up Ethan! Just shut up! You don't know anything!"

He looked at the doctor. "She imagined it, right?"

The doctor sighed. "I'm sorry, Isabelle, but he might be right."

"You can go if you want to, okay! I'm staying here!"

"You were the one who said, 'let nature take its course'! What's wrong with you now? You're such a hypocrite!" Ethan yelled.

I didn't answer and instead murmured, "Lynn, are you there? Are you still here?"

Her eyelids flickered just a little before opening. I froze.

It had to be a dream. It had to. It was just my imagination.

But then Ethan came up behind me and whispered, "You were right."

It had never felt so good to be right.

"Say something. Please," I mumbled.

My sweaty hands clutched hers, and my feet tapped violently against the ground. The beeping of the machines behind me and footsteps from outside interrupted the dead silence. Everyone was close to frozen. Ethan bit at his fingers behind me.

The doctor stared, clipboard in hand. Even he was fiddling with the pencil. And we continued to hope, for some sort of chance. Building ourselves up after we'd been torn away by Lynn's leukemia. Wishing for her to make some kind of motion that would signify that she was there.

Something to allow us to sigh and celebrate and know that our family was whole again. We held our breath.

Until finally, a strained yet powerful voice replied, "I'm here."

Epilogue

"I have to take the pills more often now," Lynn said, "To make sure I don't get too unstable again."

She was sitting on her bed, covered with a blanket, watching me doing my homework.

Mom told her to go rest, so I guess watching me doing homework was her idea of resting.

I walked over to her bed and sat beside her. "I know. But you *won't* get unstable again. I know it."

"Even if I do, I'll still pull through. For you. For all of our family."

"Yeah."

"I love you, Isa."

"Me too. And I never want you to go again." I buried my face in her shoulder.

"If anything ever happens to me again, always remember the lights. You can go wherever you want. You don't have to be held back by me. You have all your friends. Mom. Dad. Ethan—"

"Ethan's not a light," I interrupted, snorting.

She rolled her eyes. "Fine. Have it your way. But still. You have all these stars in your life, and they're beaming"

"But what about you? Surely you are also one of these 'lights,'" I said, raising my eyebrows and smirking slightly.

But Lynn doesn't take it as a joke. "There'll always be one small light that will guide you in your darkness. The light that will always be there, no matter how dim. If you keep grasping at the light, I promise, I will always be okay. No matter what happens."

Her words hit me hard, harder than she knew.

That one small light of hope. That light which I would always carry in my heart.

It would forever be Lynn's light.

Word Choice

Declan Greer worked with mentor, Beth Spencewood, on a revision focused on tweaking his word choice in his rhyming poem, *The Dragon's Curse.*

Dear Reader,

When I first read Declan's rhyming poem, *The Dragon's Curse,* I thought it was very clever that it is written as instructions on how to defeat a dragon. It's hard to find rhyming words that still fit into the flow of what you are trying to say in an interesting way, but Declan's poem manages to do both.

What Declan focused on in his revision was **choosing the best words**. Every word has the power to change the way a poem is felt by its readers so taking the time to choose unique and interesting words is time worth spending. When writing rhyming poems a lot of the focus is on the words that rhyme, but every word has the power to change the feel of the poem.

Declan looked at some of the words in the poem and made a list for each of alternate word choices. Then, he read each option out loud and chose the word he liked best. For example, in the line "Feed it meat to earn its trust" he considered the word "meat." After coming up with several options he ultimately decided to replace "meat" with

the word "boar." By specifying the kind of meat a clearer and more unique image is painted for the reader and is just that much more fun to read!

You can try this too! Choose a word in your poem or story and make a list of five to seven alternate words. They don't all have to be good, or even make that much sense! Give yourself permission to be silly with it to help open your mind to more creative options that once in a while might just be the perfect fit. Then, read the line or sentence out loud with each alternate and choose the one that you think fits and sounds best.

Have fun with your revision!

Beth Spencewood

Beth Spencewood grew up in Minneapolis, Minnesota where she spent the long winters reading her favorite books and writing short stories starring her friends. She has a bachelor's degree in psychology and worked in nonprofit management for many years. Now she has an MFA in writing and writes novels and short stories for young adults. When she isn't writing, she's playing board games, biking with her family, or cross-stitching.

Declan Greer

Declan Greer loves reading adventure novels and making freestyle LEGO creations. His favorite subject in school is library time. He has two pet cats and a little sister, and he loves to snowboard. He is also writing a science fiction novel. This is his first poem.

Beth Spencewood: What was the hardest part about writing this poem?

Declan Greer: Finding words that rhyme. Sometimes I would have to go back and change things to find a rhyming word.

Q: You said this was your first poem, what made you decide to write a poem?

A: I was reading a book about dragons and it sparked my inspiration and so I wrote one sentence and then two sentences and then I got into a groove and wrote three sentences and four sentences until I had a poem. So then I typed it and edited it and here it is.

Q: How long did it take you to write this poem?

A: That's hard to say. I started writing for about 15-20 minutes but then I took a break. Then I picked it up again a week later. And then a couple months later I saw the Inkling contest poster on the classroom window. I made some final edits and then submitted it.

Q: What are you reading right now?

A: *Harry Potter.* And I have a mountain of books left to go. And I'm listening to *39 Clues* as an audiobook so I have my hands full.

Q: What are your favorite kinds of stories?

A: That is so easy—adventure.

Q: What advice do you have for other Inklings who don't like revision very much?

A: It can be hard at first to think about different words. Just choose a word and then think about every word that you can that could work instead, and make sure to think of a lot of them so you can have choices. Then you can choose the word you like.

Q: What are you writing now or what do you plan to write next?

A: I'm currently writing an adventure novel that's pretty long. It's about Molly and Jake who are travelling to an unexplored planet when their ship catches fire. Their escape pod is the only one to land safely but Jake gets gobbled up by river monsters and Molly has to save him. The book is about them trying to get back home.

The Dragon's
Curse

by

Declan Greer

Beware, beware of the dragon's lair,
Kidnaps princesses kind and fair.
Who will slay the beast of fire,
And rule a terrific empire?
And yet, you should heed my warning,
its whelps will emerge in the morning,
If you attempt to slay the beast,
You'll become a dragon feast,
Because it needs to feed it's kin,
They'll drink your blood and eat your skin

If you're not a coward but brave,
Enter in the mouth of the cave.
Stalactites, stalagmites, piles of bones,
It's your only chance to take the throne.
Tame it, tame it, if you must,

Feed it boar to earn its trust,

And then, at the end of the day,

The dragon's power is at bay.

But, you see, that's not the end,

For the dragon's curse no one can defend.

Not armor, not words,

Not magical birds.

And well, since dragons like to hoard,

with it's loot you'll be a lord!

with this gold you'll start to brag,

the dragon's curse you'll start to snag.

you'll stop being all polite and kind.

"I rule the world," you'll think in your mind.

it just keeps on getting worse, the unstoppable greed,

keeps you from defining your wants from your needs.

So are you going to change your mind,

stop resisting the greed but leave your whole life behind?

well, that choice is one *you* have to make,

decide if that's a risk you want to take.

Point of View

Claire Belcourt worked with mentor, Jamie Kallio, on a revision focused on point of view in Claire's work of historical fiction, *Rue Saint Paul.*

Dear Reader,

Everyone has a point of view, and every writer must choose a **point of view** from which to tell her story. Claire's story, *Rue St. Paul,* is based on an actual historical event. In real life, the testimony of a five-year-old girl determined the outcome of this event. Claire uses the little girl as her 3rd person narrator, Lydia.

When Claire and I met for revision of Rue St. Paul, we both realized that Lydia had a very sophisticated vocabulary for a little girl. Claire thought about making the narrator older, but she wanted to remain true to the real event. The challenge for Claire was to find a way to tell this story, without missing any of the crucial details, but making Lydia's voice sound true for her age.

We discussed the point of view in several of Claire's favorite books; were they in 1st person or 3rd ? We talked about which point of view she naturally gravitated to in her own writing. We played around with the idea of Lydia telling the story from 1st person, but Claire wondered if being so close inside a child's head would water down

the harsh details of this important story. Then we discussed another approach: Lydia could remember the incident as a grown woman, much like the narrator Scout in *To Kill A Mockingbird*. Taking this approach would allow Claire to keep a level of sophistication in her story.

In the end, Claire decided to keep Lydia as a five-year-old and focused on changing her language in the story. She also dug deeper into sensory details and into Lydia's childlike reasoning. This choice, as you will see, turned out to be the right one.

If you ever find yourself struggling with point of view, you might try what Claire did: think about your favorite books. What are the points of view? Why do you like them? In your own work, if you changed point of view, how might the entire story change? And what feels most natural to you?

Rue Saint Paul will grab hold of you right from the beginning and won't let go until the breathtaking end.

I hope you love it as much as I do.

Jamie Kallio

Jamie Kallio is a writer and librarian in the south suburbs of Chicago. She has an MFA in writing for children and young adults from Hamline University, and an MFA in the teaching of writing from Columbia College, Chicago. She is the author of many nonfiction books for children. Historical fiction is her favorite of all the genres.

Claire Belcourt

Claire Belcourt is in seventh grade at Duke of Connaught Public School in Ontario. You can often find her watching basketball or listening to music. She frequents Japanese food restaurants and the beach near her house. She likes skateboarding, the ocean/lake, writing, mythology, long car rides, travelling around her province, her pets, and history. Her interest in history led her to find the case of Marie-Joseph Angelique, and later on inspired her to write *Rue Saint Paul*.

Jamie Kallio: How did you come up with your story idea?

Claire Belcourt: A year ago, I did a history fair project on something I thought was very interesting—the case of Marie-Joseph Angelique. My friend and I were researching mysteries in Canadian history, and found that a female slave in 1734, Marie-Joseph Angelique, was accused of setting a fire that burned forty-five houses and one hospital with no proof except a five-year-old girl. We did our project on this topic. So, when I was brainstorming ideas for a story, this case popped up in my brain. I knew I had to write about it but couldn't figure out who should be the main character. Then, I remembered that there was a five year old girl who testified, and I knew I had to write this story, and the five-year-old girl had to be the main character.

Q: Where do you like to write?

A: I cannot tell you how many hours I've spent sitting on my bed, writing. My bed is my safe space, and I can block out the noise of my house in my room. In the summer, I like to open my window to let a breeze in, and I can visualise

an outdoor scene better as well. Sometimes, if I'm lucky, my cat will come and sleep on my lap. I'm sure you've heard the saying don't work where you sleep, but writing isn't work for me, especially when I'm in a place like my bed where I feel comfortable and inspired.

Q: What are your favorite books and why?

A: When I was a little younger, I passed by a cardboard box with a sign that said 'Books for sale' and looked through it. I was caught by the bright red apple on the cover of *Twilight* and took it home. When I started to read the book, I truly could not put it down, and at that age, I hadn't experienced that feeling before. A little while after that, I started to write my first story and really get into books. My favourite book now, however, is *To Kill a Mockingbird*. I had to read it for school, but it didn't feel like schoolwork as I was completely caught in the plot and beautiful message. Harper Lee did a wonderful job of creating characters and conveying an important message, which is why it's a book that has stuck with me for so long and will be one of my favorite books forever.

Q: What surprised you about the rewriting process?

A: I was pretty familiar with rewriting a story as I have submitted other books before, but I was still surprised with how I truly managed to not take any notes to heart. I think it's important in the rewriting process to not take offense to anything that someone says, and that they are only trying to make your story better. This wasn't only because I had learned this lesson from rewriting before—I must mention how fantastic my contest mentor was. She really made this process easy for me and allowed me to choose what I would revise at the end of the day, which really let me shine.

Q: How did you chose the ending to your story?

A: I hadn't had this ending in my head while I was writing the majority of my story. Initially, I was going to write in my main character testifying and would choose if she would go against her parents or not. I'm a very indecisive person, so as I got closer and closer to finishing, I still hadn't made up my mind on which way to go. That's when I had my idea—the readers didn't have to know at the end of the day if the main character went against her parents, because the point of the story was to show a young girl navigating through a major life event and opening her eyes to the fact that everything isn't black and white; you can't always know right from wrong. Once I had this idea, I was much happier with my plot and my story in general.

Rue Saint Paul

by

Claire Belcourt

Based on a real story

In her short five years of life, Lydia had heard of uncontrollable fires, but she could never have imagined how devastating and monstrous it was in person.

It was a nice spring day in 1734. April had just arrived in Montreal, bringing its light breeze and colourful flowers. The month normally also meant rain, however there hadn't been any for a few weeks and the bright blue sky showed no hints of that changing.

Usually, when Lydia was coming back from religion class, she would be admiring the newly sprouted buds on the edges of the trees she'd walk by. She would sing a song for herself or look at expensive houses she wished she had, to pass the five minutes or so it took to get home, and look up at the cloudless blue sky.

But on that day, Lydia felt rebellious, and decided to take a longer route through Rue Saint Paul to avoid getting home and being forced to do her

chores. It was such a nice day, and she wanted to play outside during her walk before cleaning the chicken coop. Rue Saint Paul was full of wealthy families that she was sure didn't make their children do any chores, and she wanted to pretend to be one of those lucky kids, even just for the couple of minutes it took to pass the street.

She had expected to see beautiful, lush maple and spruce trees, but most of the trees Lydia could see were on fire, shooting sparks into the air. Instead of seeing notably large, intricate houses, Lydia noticed that one part of the row of houses was completely engulfed while others were rapidly burning. The house that was fully consumed by the blazing fire was the one that she admired the most. It was the biggest and most grandiose on the entire street, but as Lydia looked at it, it was just bones of the house it used to be. Billows of smoke filled the sky, casting a dark cloud over Rue Saint Paul and sinking into Lydia's lungs as she coughed profusely. The sound of the roaring fire was almost able to mask the loud crashes of parts of houses falling that Lydia heard.

She had always wished she lived in a house like the ones that were now aflame. Lydia would pass these houses pretty often, every time imagining playing in a room that was hers, with a comfortable bed and as many toys as she could ever want instead of her small bed cramped in the corner of her parent's room. She would wonder if the houses' owners knew how lucky they were.

Tears rushed down Lydia's cheeks as she tried to find someone-- anyone—that could help her, but she was utterly alone. Her stomach turned as she suddenly felt very small.

"Help!" Lydia screamed, turning her back to the fire. "Can somebody do something?" She couldn't stand to watch the houses she had fantasized about living in be turned to ash.

She ran. She could hear neighbours escaping their houses, horses pulling hose wagons, and children screaming. People were falling in a panic, desperately attempting to get to safety and horses panicked as their owners lost control of them. This horrified Lydia, but also fueled her to run faster, away from the fire, towards her safe home and into her mother's embrace. Finally, the sounds started to drain away, first to a mere whisper, then to just a sound that wouldn't stop echoing in Lydia's mind.

The houses got smaller and smaller until Lydia finally reached her house. It wasn't grand or big like the houses she had been amongst a few minutes ago, but there was nowhere else she would rather be. She threw open the door as fast as she could and scanned the room for her mother, but she wasn't there. Panic seeped into Lydia as more tears filled her eyes.

"Mama? Where are you?" Lydia called, barely able to get her words out through her sobs.

She wanted more than anything to see her mother and feel safe after so much time of being alone and helpless. Of course, it hadn't truly been that long but it had felt like days to Lydia.

"Are you here?"

Lydia's mother, Elizabeth, came rushing down the stairs with a broom in her hand.

"Yes, Lydia?" Her mother asked with a slightly bothered tone that vanished when she saw Lydia's face. "My goodness, what happened?"

"Th—there was a fire. I saw it coming back from religion class, and no one was there to help me! It was so large, it took up at least five houses." Lydia managed, wiping the tears from her face.

"Are you all right? Let's get you cleaned up."

Lydia looked down at her dress, which was covered in ash from the fire. There were also tiny burn marks which were from sparks coming off from

the fire. When Lydia had been near the fire and running away, she hadn't noticed any of her surroundings, other than how many houses were completely engulfed in flames.

"I'm okay. Yes, I guess I got my dress dirty. I'm sorry," Lydia apologized, hoping her mother wouldn't get upset for how poorly Lydia had taken care of her best dress. It was strictly reserved for her religion class and any special events that might require fancy attire. Not that Lydia had ever needed a nice dress--her parents were never invited to any balls. The only parties they went to were at taverns or alehouses. Lydia had once asked her mother why they never went to any of the balls that Lydia had heard about, but her mother had laughed and said, "No one would invite us to a fancy event. I mean, look at our house, honey. It's not like the ones on Rue Saint Paul, that's for sure."

Her mother's voice snapped Lydia back into reality. "No, no, no. There's no need to worry. It's just important that you're all right. Do you remember where this was?"

"I do. It was at Rue Saint Paul," Lydia stated, starting up the stairs with her mother.

"Oh! With all the nice houses? Really?"

"Yes, I know. It looked awful, especially with how big all the houses are. But I heard the hose wagons coming after I started coming home. I think it will be okay."

Her mother wiped Lydia's face with a wet dish rag. "Oh, yes, I'm sure it'll be fine. Don't worry about it, all right?"

"All right, I won't. I promise," Lydia reassured her, knowing very well that she was lying. She was completely aware that this would stay with her for a long time.

Lydia came downstairs, excited for the day ahead of her. It was Sunday, so both of her parents were home. Lydia was looking forward to her father reading her the newspaper over breakfast. They would discuss everything that he read.

However, that morning, Lydia came downstairs to find the newspaper sitting on the dining table and her parents eating in silence. Neither of them said anything to Lydia as she took her seat.

A few minutes after Lydia finished her breakfast, her father spoke.

"So I saw in the paper that there was a fire. Your mother said you passed by it while you were walking home. Is that true?"

"Yes. It was huge. Did the firefighters manage to get rid of it?" Lydia asked.

Her father looked down at the table. "The firefighters did put out the fire, but many houses were lost, along with a hospital. It was devastating." He looked at Lydia and saw the look of worry on her face. "But what matters is that the fire is out."

Lydia's mother spoke next. "Did you see anyone there, honey? Near the fire?"

"No," Lydia said, "I don't think so. I didn't get a great look, but I'm pretty sure there wasn't anyone."

"Of course you had to have seen someone! The houses didn't light themselves," Lydia's father said with a nervous chuckle under his breath.

"I really don't think so," started Lydia, "I mean, I could have missed someone, but no one tried to help me. Most people would try to."

"Maybe whoever did this didn't want to be found. If I were to commit arson, I certainly wouldn't want to be caught," Lydia's mother said from the closet-sized pantry just behind the kitchen and dining room.

Would someone really ignore a child during a fire to avoid getting caught? Lydia thought. *They would have to be a really awful person.*

Lydia's dad then said, "That's a good point, Elizabeth. I can only imagine what the person who did this would be like. I wouldn't put that past them. If you can set houses on fire, I bet that you'd have no problem leaving a small child alone near it."

As the day passed, Lydia couldn't stop thinking about the conversation she had with her parents. What kind of person would leave a child so dangerously close to a fire? Maybe they hadn't meant to start the fire, but once they had, they needed to run away. Maybe they *were* a bad person who wanted to cause trouble, however the fire was made much larger and more dangerous than they had ever wanted it to be. Or maybe there just was no one there at all.

Before Lydia knew it, she woke up again to a new day. Once again, something seemed wrong. When she awoke, her father and mother stepped up to her bed. They were both well-dressed and ready for the new day.

"Good morning, Lydia," her mother chimed, sitting on the edge of her bed. "It's a wonderful day, no?"

Turning her head to look out her window, Lydia noticed how bright and cheerful it was outside. The chirps of birds filled the room.

"Yes, it is. Is everything okay?"

Lydia's father walked closer to her bed. "Of course! We have good news."

He paused, perhaps to build anticipation. He didn't wait for Lydia to ask what news he was talking about. "The police have found the person who set the fire! Her name is Marie Joseph-Angelique, a slave of the homeowner."

Her mother looked out the window, then asked, "Did you see a female slave anywhere near the fire? I'm sure you would have had to, the police are sure that she committed the arson."

"How do they know it was her?" Lydia asked, deflecting.

She knew that she hadn't seen anyone, but there was still the possibility

that someone had been hiding. She didn't want to believe that anyone would purposefully set the houses on fire.

"The slave talked back to her master all the time, threatening to burn the house down to the ground. It got so bad that Marie's master had to sell her to someone else—she couldn't take it anymore! And that's when Marie burnt down the house," her mother explained.

"So they're sure?" Lydia questioned, "She's going to jail?"

"Well, not yet. There's going to be a trial, of course," her father said. "She will be taken before a judge and witnesses will tell their stories. If she is found guilty, there's no doubt she'll be taken to jail, or worse,"

Lydia didn't have time to think about what worse could possibly be, she wanted to know more. "Where were these people who saw Marie set the fire? Why didn't they help me?"

"A few people were there. Perhaps they didn't see you," Lydia's mother explained, "Neighbours and whatnot. However, you were there first, and you saw a good deal of it. That's why we want you to testify. We've already told the police, but we want you to be sure that you saw Marie."

Both Lydia's mother and father looked at her expectantly. Even though her mother made it seem like it was a question, Lydia was aware that she didn't have much of a choice. She would have to testify, and her parents would make her say that she saw a female slave near the fire, whether or not Lydia really did.

They could only want what was best for her, right? If they were sure that Marie Joseph-Angelique had set the fire, she must have. Why would her parents lie about that?

"I can do that. If you think I should testify, I will," Lydia said. She was ready for her parents to thank her or make some sort of mention of how well she was behaving, but it never came. It was typical--she knew her parents loved

her and were just too busy to pay much attention to her, but every once in a while it felt like she was doing everything she could to make them happy and still was never good enough. This made whatever attention she did get very special, and she thought that agreeing to testify would help her get this prized praise, but it seemed as if that wasn't going to happen.

Her thoughts were interrupted by the scream of a woman from outside.

Lydia, along with her parents, raced down the stairs to see what was happening. Her father flung open the door. On the street in front of their house, a woman was struggling against two policemen who were trying to handcuff her.

"Please, you have to understand! I didn't do a thing. They're all lying, I'm telling you!" The woman shouted.

She battled against the policemen so hard that a piece of her dress ripped from under one of the policemen's shoe.

A considerably large group of people had gathered to watch this, more people adding to the crowd by the second. Some people called this woman names that Lydia didn't even know the meaning of. Some people whispered to the people beside them, and some people, like Lydia, stood and watched in horror.

Who is this woman? Why do so many people know of her? She thought, until something clicked.

"Mama?" Lydia called, tugging on her mother's dress.

Her mother looked down at her. "Yes?"

"Is this…" Lydia looked up again at the woman, whose hands were now finally in the handcuffs. "Is this Marie? The slave you were talking about earlier?"

"Yes, honey. It is."

Lydia watched as the police pulled Marie further away from their

house, presumably towards the jailhouse. As they were taking her away, Marie looked behind her, right at Lydia, her eyes pleading, glassy with tears. It seemed like the whole world stopped.

Lydia stared at Marie, wondering why anyone would think her guilty. She didn't look evil. She didn't look dirty or like a monster. She just looked human.

The gallery was filled with people Lydia knew. Some were neighbours, some were family friends, some were people from her religion class. A few people waved politely at her, maybe said hello, but no one started a conversation. Lydia was smart enough to understand that this was because they wanted to see Marie-Joseph Angelique be found guilty and punished. People were careful, no one would want to be associated with someone who defended a slave. Everyone thought about slaves as monsters, an idea that Lydia was starting to question.

Lydia and her parents sat in one of the many rows inside the courtroom. In front of her she saw a desk that seemed as tall as her house. Her mother explained that this was where the judge would sit. Lydia would be in the witness stand next to him. He would undoubtedly be staring her down the entire time she was bearing witness.

Lydia turned to look behind her. The courtroom doors opened and in walked Marie, accompanied by two policemen on either side of her. Her hands and feet were shackled and she looked like she hadn't slept for days.

It had been an entire week since Lydia had seen Marie being taken by the police, and it hadn't once left her mind. She knew she had to make a decision about what she would say. If she hadn't held eye contact with Marie a week ago, she would never have thought about it twice.

She would have told the lie her parents wanted her to. They went over what she was to say again and again to make sure she wouldn't mess up. However, after seeing the raw desperation behind Marie's eyes, Lydia wasn't so sure.

Lydia knew that there wasn't enough time to think about it. She would be testifying in a few minutes' time, either to admit that she'd seen no one and disappoint her family, or lie and watch a possibly innocent woman go to prison. A decision needed to be made, but all she did was watch time on the clock pass by. She'd been waiting thirty seconds. A minute. Two minutes. Three. Four…

She heard her name called. Sitting up, Lydia looked at everyone as they watched her, eyes peeled. Her legs took her up to the witness stand. A clerk with thinning grey hair came up to her and laid a Bible on the ledge of the witness stand.

"Place your right hand on the bible and raise your left hand," he ordered as Lydia struggled to reach her hand all the way to the ledge where the Bible lay.

It took a few seconds, but Lydia stretched her arm high enough to touch the Bible. She traced her finger along the worn leather, thinking of how many other people had been standing right where she was then. Her left arm shook with nervousness as she waited for further instruction.

The clerk held stark cold eye contact with Lydia. "Repeat after me. Do you solemnly swear that you will tell the truth, the whole truth, and nothing but the truth, so help you God?"

Lydia closed her eyes, just for a moment, to regather her thoughts. Without a clear mind, she knew she'd say something she'd regret. She knew she had to do as she was told, but what if she decided that she'd say she did see Marie at the fire after swearing to be truthful? Whatever or whoever was above her, watching over her, what would they think of that?

Then, she looked at her family as they pleaded with their eyes. "I

solemnly swear to tell the truth…" her little voice managed, quietly, but still said.

She looked at Marie, who was looking out of the courthouse window longingly, as if Lydia wasn't speaking at all. "The whole truth…" she continued, this time beholding everyone in the gallery. They all stared at her, no doubt wanting to see what Lydia would say after this. Would she confirm that Marie was guilty and be accepted by the people around her? Or would she stand up against everyone else's beliefs and assumptions?

"And nothing but the truth."

She was ready--she needed no other time to think. A decision in her mind had been made. As soon as she was done with her oath, she would reveal this decision to every spectator in that courthouse.

"So help me God."

Setting for Tone

Claire Guo worked with mentor, Beth Spencewood, on a revision of Claire's story, *The Road She Walked*, focused on deeping tone using setting details.

Dear Reader,

All stories happen somewhere, and the way that place is described impacts the way the reader feels while they read it. Claire's winning story builds a beautiful place for her character's story to unfold. It is full of lush, elegant details that really brings it to life. The beauty her character sees in the world was evident at every turn.

What Claire worked on for this revision was **using her setting to control the tone of the story**. The way a moment in a story feels can change dramatically depending on the way the setting is described. Is the light through the window bright and cheerful or is it harsh and illuminating?

Using the way your character feels guide the words you choose to describe the setting helps control the tone of the piece. It can also give the

reader crucial insight into how the character is feeling.

To do this revision Claire listed the way Daphne felt in each scene and then used that feeling to inform the way the setting around her was described. This is most evident in the scene in the park. See if you can spot how the way the park is described changes throughout the scene and what that change tells you about how Daphne is feeling after she goes through a difficult event.

If you want to try to use your setting to control the tone in your story, first start by listing how your character feels in each scene and how it changes. Then look at the way the setting is described and ask yourself if it lines up with those feelings. If not, brainstorm other details about the setting and look for ones that align with the tone of that moment.

Happy writing!

Beth Spencewood

Beth Spencewood grew up in Minneapolis, Minnesota where she spent the long winters reading her favorite books and writing short stories starring her friends. She has a bachelor's degree in psychology and worked in nonprofit management for many years. Now she has an MFA in writing and writes novels and short stories for young adults. When she isn't writing, she's playing board games, biking with her family, or cross-stitching.

Claire Guo

Claire Guo lives in San Jose, California and is in sixth grade, where her favorite subject is language arts. She has a twin sister who is also a writer. When she isn't writing, Claire enjoys reading fantasy, doing any kind of crafting, drawing, and traveling. The Road She Walked is the first piece of hers to be published. Claire also loves to write poetry. Her favorite food is mango sorbet.

Beth Spencewood: What was the hardest part about writing this story?

Claire Guo: The hardest part was coming up with the idea for it. I was considering writing fantasy or something that wasn't in the real world. This one was easier to run with. The words came more naturally and I kept typing and typing until I had the story.

Q: What kinds of stories do you like to write most?

A: I like to write this style and also fantasy.

Q: What advice do you have for other Inklings who don't like revision very much?

A: It's more fun than it looks. And more fun than it sounds. When you are done revising it feels really good because you look over your story and it sounds so much better than before.

Q: What are you writing now or what do you plan to write next?

A: I plan on writing for different writing contests. I also want to write a book. I'm hoping to write a few pages each day and one day have a book that I can sell. I just wrote a dystopian story about a world that had been infected by disease. The main character wasn't able to go outside because the virus was in the air. There is a virus suit you can get but only the government and officials can afford it. But she thinks everyone should be able to have one so she uncovers the lies that the government was telling that was keeping them from everyone.

Q: What are you reading right now?

A: I'm reading the *Throne of Glass* Series. I'm also waiting for the next *Keeper of the Lost Cities* series. I have a lot of favorites but those are among them.

The Road She Walked

by

Claire Guo

The morning came with a leaky roof.

Daphne glanced upwards, watching a small drizzle of rain trickle slowly through the ceiling of her run-down trailer and onto the floor, sliding delicately down the diagonal table like children on a slide. The sun, washing the earth with a golden glow, was hidden behind the skirts of puffy black and grey clouds. She moved to the table, where a half-eaten McDonalds burger lay soaked in a puddle of water, and wrinkled her nose in distaste, wondering where she would get her food that day. Anger and anxiety sank in, reaching through her body to her toes, but she shook it off with a shiver.

Wandering out of the trailer, Daphne decided to take a walk in the rain, as the sun would surely come out in an hour or two. She listened to the patter of the rain as she walked, row after row of scavenged tents and old cars soon behind her in the pale sky. Forward, the city lay, buildings galloping up to the clouds. Yet she did not run, though the feelings were starting to creep forward, like a shadow she could never really shake.

A mile later, she stood at a forest trail.

And now she ran, feet kissing the dirt, pounding on the floor and the rhythm washes away the thoughts. The sweat, tears, pulse: she relished the feeling. She ran as though she was born to run, to travel as fast as sound and swift as a cheetah, and she ran until the thoughts were gone and the depression had long since faded.

By now the rain had stopped, revealing a blue sky and sun, speckled with arcs of black like ink from the quill of a pen, but they were birds. The smell of nature swept through her nose, fragrant and sweet. Daphne was struck, in a moment, by the tranquility of the sky, and the serenity of the clouds. The city sprawls the valley below.

She turned around and walked back down the trail.

This was the end of her road.

As Daphne walked back to the camp, she passed a small, cozy park, nothing like the ones near the city. This one was not arranged, yet had flowers more vibrant than all the varieties. She passed a white tiled fountain shooting jets of rainbow reflected water, and the head of a beautiful duck too. Surprisingly, it was empty.

Daphne walked in.

Entering the park, a slight breeze brought petals pirouetting to the grass. She bent down, scooping a handful and letting their perfume waft through her nose. The park was enchanting, full of roses and asters and lilies. She smiled and walked to the fountain in the middle.

Spurting water, the delicate fountain displayed several tiers, each surrounded with a layer of blue tiles. She trailed hand in the crystal blue waters, and leaning forward, caught a glimpse of her reflection.

Strands of flyaway black hair danced in the wind, and dirt smudges from her hike coated areas of her face. She tugged self-consciously at her

shabby clothes and worn shoes, eyeing a small mole on her neck with a tinge of despair. She looked terrible, smelled terrible, but still she felt great. There was something calming about the park, something she could not pin down. Sitting on a bench, Daphne closed her eyes, letting her senses explore.

The smells... She could smell the scent of aromatic flowers, and the sounds were the pleasant chirp of birds and the gurgle of the fountain. Once in a while, a petal would graze her skin. Daphne sighed happily, thinking she should visit more often.

Then there was the sound of yelling, and her eyelids snapped open. The birds stopped singing, and the trees stopped swaying. Whipping around, she saw a red-faced man running at her with a rake. The man must have known she was homeless.

"Get out of this park! You aren't allowed to sleep here!" He yelled.

Daphne gasped, and ran out, crying.

Suddenly the flowers seemed to be laughing, and the tall white gate that had looked so ornate now looked dangerous and looming. She could no longer hear the sounds of nature, only the sound of her own labored breathing and the man's shouts. Desperately, she held onto the good feelings from before, but all she could think of was the feeling of loss, and the garden that now felt like a treacherous land.

She quickened her pace and sped to camp, the tears streaming down like a fountain, like the fountain in the garden that used to feel like home.

Nighttime drew upon her like a shadow, with crickets chirping and the buzz of flies. Drop after drop of water dripped down to the dirty, muddy floor. She could not sleep, her mind whirling with anxiety and sadness. Getting up quietly, she slipped on a thin jacket.

As Daphne walked out of the camp, her home, the only light came

from the moon and the dirty lamp posts mustering feeble glows. Silvery moonbeams illuminated the uneven sidewalk. Throughout the neighborhood, the sounds of her shoe against concrete echoed quietly. She could not help but replay the moments in the park. Before long, she broke down, crying.

Daphne was so stressed, and the weight seemed to be a rock over her heart, and it was never gone. Never, ever, gone. Sometimes she could not lift her head, could not sleep, could not think, could not eat. She wanted a life, a better one: she wanted to have a home.

Weeping, Daphne cried for the future she would never have, and all her dreams, all that she loved, everything she had hoped for vanished with her tears. Like rivers, they spilled down her cheeks, and only stopped when she drew a breath of air.

Suddenly, her tears quieted.

In front of her was a patch of trees, thick, gnarly branches like fingers clawing the silky night. The roots seemed to snake through the earth. For a moment she was scared, until her eyes caught sight of an opening in the trees, where there was a track. It was decorated with pristine white lines and smooth cut grass. Her breath caught in her throat. It was the school track, lined with silver bleachers, brightened by one powerful light and silent in the pitch black. Daphne's heart tumbled over itself.

Her heart was weighed down by sadness, by just a tiny part itched to run. She closed her eyes, the exhilaration, joy, and anticipation from her morning run speeding through her. Her right foot moved forward an inch, but her left foot kept her grounded, stuck onto her despair and sadness. Until she remembered her passion for running. She could no longer stay still. She leapt through pointy bushes and onto the field. And she ran.

She ran and ran and ran.

She ran as though she could outrun life, pounding feet on the grass and flying over the floor. She ran like the waves on the shore and lightning when it reaches the trees. She ran like water and wind and fire and earth. She ran for the life in her blood.

Slowly, she sputtered to a stop, panting and heaving, chest burning, and walked for a minute to slow her furious heart rate. The tears were gone now; only adrenaline remained coursing through her veins. Beaded perspiration lay glistening on her forehead; rosy red outlined her cheeks. Daphne felt renewed, focusing on the sound of her lungs, expanding and contracting to her steps.

And then someone clapped.

She spun around, horrified.

An athletic lady with a perfect build was walking from the shadows of the bleachers. She waved a hand in greeting and nodded her head with a smirk. She clapped again, and nearing, patted the girl on the shoulder.

"You're just the person we need." She announced.

Her name was Alyssa, and she was a track and field coach. She was missing a star runner for her team. Alyssa was willing to accept Daphne, free of charge. Daphne was astounded.

Daphne felt as though she were glowing, the track around her a shower of crystal lights. The world seemed to be racing, the lights casting a blossoming beam around her. Something inside her clicked, and now the track felt like home when she scuffed her heel on the wet, dewy grass.

This was not the end of the road for her, for she could be a runner. She had never once considered the possibility, yet now, it was so clear.

Breaking her out of her thoughts, Alyssa asked, "Where do you live?"

Daphne blushed, deep red highlighting her still red cheeks. A stone plunked into her stomach. She wondered what she should say, what would happen if she said, and how the expression on Alyssa's kindly face would change.

"I'm homeless." Daphne whispered.

Alyssa's smile melted into shock, her mouth set in a silent *o*, and Daphne gasped as Alyssa reached over to hug her tightly. She rested her head on Alyssa's shoulder, her chin trembling like a small child's. A single silent tear traveled down her cheek, splashing onto the track.

This was the beginning of a new road.